HOW COME THE BEST CLUES ARE ALWAYS IN THE GARBAGE?

HOW COME THE BEST CLUES ARE ALWAYS IN THE GARBAGE?

Linda Bailey

KIDS CAN PRESS LTD.
TORONTO

Kids Can Press Ltd. acknowledges with appreciation the assistance of the Canada Council and the Ontario Arts Council in the production of this book.

Canadian Cataloguing in Publication Data

Bailey, Linda, 1948-
How come the best clues are always in the garbage?

ISBN 1-55074-094-6

I. Title.

PS8553.A55H68 1992   jC813'.54   C92-093435-8
PZ7.B35Ho 1992

Kids Can Press Ltd.
29 Birch Avenue
Toronto, Ontario, Canada
M4V 1E2

Edited by Charis Wahl
Cover design by N. R. Jackson
Interior design by Esperança Melo

Printed and bound in Canada

92 0 9 8 7 6 5 4 3

For Lia and Tess, with love and thanks
for their many ideas

CHAPTER

I STARTED MY CAREER AS A FAMOUS DETECTIVE ON A bright and windy day in early October. Up until the robbery, it was the most ordinary day a girl ever spent. Peanut butter sandwich for lunch, floor hockey in gym, spiders in science...

See what I mean? Snore.

And me? I was a perfectly regular kid. Stephanie Olivia Diamond, sixth grader. New girl at Emily Carr Elementary School. Most days, you could catch me walking around with my nose in a book. I also liked to collect comics and bake chocolate macaroons and paint my sneakers with fabric paint. Like I said, pretty regular. I didn't even know I *wanted* to be a detective.

That was then. By the time it was all over, I was practically a hero. One newspaper said I was "Vancouver's answer to Nancy Drew." Another one called me a "girl wonder."

Me, a girl wonder... can you imagine?

It all started when I came home from school and found my mom collapsed in the old green chair. I could see right away she'd been crying.

Most people, when they've been crying, their eyes get red. With my mom, it's her nose. So there she was, collapsed in a heap, with a nose as bright as Rudolph's and a bunch of balled-up toilet paper clutched in her hand. She hardly even glanced up when I came in.

"Mom? What's wrong?"

For a minute, I was scared something had happened to my dad. He's been up in the Yukon for months, doing research on mountain goats, so he can get a Master's degree in biology. Maybe he'd been attacked by a grizzly bear, maybe—

"It's the money. It's been stolen. Someone broke into our place while I was out. Stephanie, the money's gone!" My mom's voice was little and quivery.

"What? You mean the Garbage Busters' money?"

She nodded. I plopped down on the couch so hard the springs bounced.

This was bad. Garbage Busters is this environmental group my mom works for. It tries to get people to recycle and cut down on their garbage and make compost bins. It's not big like Greenpeace, and it doesn't have much money. That's why we'd been so excited when people donated all that cash—more than a thousand dollars—at the Walk for the Environment the day before. My mom had brought the money home, and we'd been up till almost midnight counting it and rolling up the coins.

"I can't believe it!" I said. "You were going to put it in the bank today. What happened?"

Well. That *really* got her going. The tears poured

down her face like it was a water fountain.

"It's all my fault," she said after a while, in that shaky little voice—nothing like her regular voice, which I can hear easily a block away when she's looking for me. "I had it all laid out on the kitchen table. The bills in stacks and all the rolls of coins in a row. I was just about to take it to the bank and then—"

I waited while she blew her nose and wiped her face. She looked kind of embarrassed now.

"I went for a bike ride," she said finally. "Jonathon came by and invited me to go biking along the ocean. It was such a lovely day, and I...well, I just went off and left all that money sitting there. Right out in the open. Right where anybody—"

"Mom!" I interrupted. "You went out with Jonathon? *Again?*"

For the first time that afternoon, she sat up and looked like her old self. Like a mom, that is.

"Stephanie, *why* don't you like Jonathon? He's been wonderful. If it hadn't been for him, we never would have gotten this town house. You know how hard it is to get into housing co-ops these days. It was only because he lived here and knew about the vacancy—"

"Yeah, I know." I was glad that we weren't still living in that awful basement with the drippy walls. "It's just—well, does he have to hang around so much?"

"Sweetie, we're lucky to get volunteers at Garbage Busters, and Jonathon puts in a lot of hours. He's a whiz at the accounting and financial stuff.

9

We ought to be grateful that..."

I stopped listening, thinking instead about the *real* reason I don't like Jonathon. It's because of how he looks. Handsome enough to be a movie star. And way, *way* handsomer than my dad. When Jonathon smiles, he shines about a hundred big white teeth right at you—you practically need sunglasses to look at them. And he's got so many muscles you can see them right through those stretchy exercise suits he wears.

My dad—to be perfectly honest—is not handsome at all. He always looks sort of goofy, like somebody should brush his hair or something. I don't think he even *tries* to be handsome.

None of this would matter, of course, if my dad were here in Vancouver. But with him thousands of miles away, it was only a matter of time. One of these days, my mom would take a good look at Jonathon. And then, kaboom! First, she'd Fall in Love, and then she'd Get Divorced, and then she'd Get Married to Jonathon and, well...you see my point. Goodbye, Dad.

My mom was still babbling on about Jonathon. "And today he was so helpful with the police. It's not easy for me, with your dad away, and—"

"Mom, can you *stop* talking about Jonathon for just a second? You haven't even told me what happened. Did you leave the door unlocked?"

"Of course not!" She looked shocked, and I decided not to mention all the times I had gone out and left the door unlocked when she was at work. "That's what's so crazy. I locked the door, and then Jonathon and I went biking down to

Granville Island. We stopped for tea and watched the pigeons, and when we got back the money was — was — " My mom's voice caught, like it was full of tears.

"Gone?" I said helpfully.

She nodded. "Gone."

Radical, our cat, strolled into the living room and leaped onto my lap. He thinks of it as his own personal cat-sized chair. I gave him a scratch behind the ears while I thought about what my mom had said.

"What about the police, Mom? I bet they'll track down the thief in no time, and then — "

She shook her head and sighed. "They were here this afternoon, asking me and Jonathon all kinds of questions. They were nice, but they said they don't have much to go on. Seems like there's not much hope of getting the money back."

"Did you tell them about the phone calls?"

"What phone calls?"

I couldn't believe it. She hadn't even told them about the phone calls.

"Mom!" I said. "The weird calls we've been getting for the last two weeks! The ones where we pick up the phone and the person on the other end hangs up."

"Oh, those," she said. "I told you, Steph, it's just kids fooling around. It has nothing to do with this." But I could tell by her face — she was thinking about it, all right.

I'd been telling her all along it wasn't kids. Kids might make one phone call, but they wouldn't keep it up this long. Besides, one of the calls had come really late at night, when kids are asleep.

"Mom? Did you ever hear anything on the calls?"

"No." She looked worried. "Why?"

"I'm not sure. There was this faint sound once—on that call that came in the middle of the night."

"Oh, dear," she muttered. "I wish you'd waited for me to answer."

"I did," I said. "I waited at least ten rings. But you sleep like a rock, Mom. You sleep like *ten* rocks."

"Never mind that now. What did you hear?"

"I don't know. It wasn't very loud. Not a voice. But something familiar. Some sound I've definitely heard before."

She sat up straight, looking so nervous I was sorry I'd mentioned it. "I can't take it," she said suddenly. "Mysterious phone calls, thieves breaking into my house in broad daylight—"

Uh, oh. She was going to start bawling again. Dumping Radical on the floor, I went over to give her a hug. "Poor Mom," I said, snuggling into the green chair beside her.

She put her arm around my shoulder. "Oh, honey, I'm sorry. It's just that—well, this isn't great for my job, you know."

I knew, all right. I knew that Garbage Busters was having trouble paying my mom her salary. This would make it even worse. Maybe she wouldn't have her job much longer.

"Mrroow!" Radical was still right where I'd dropped him. He was giving me just about the grumpiest look a cat can give a person. "Mrroow," he repeated and marched—as well as a cat can

12

march, that is—straight over to the green chair. He leaped back onto my lap and lay down as if he owned it. *There*, he seemed to say, *I dare you to move*.

The green chair was pretty crowded now, but cozy at the same time. The three of us sat there together for a while, with me and my mom thinking about the robbery and Radical probably thinking about the yummy bowl of Kitty Chow he was going to have for dinner. As the minutes rolled by, I started to have a whole bunch of different feelings about the robbery.

First, I felt sad. And scared, too. What if my mom lost her job? Not that we've ever had much money, but I know what it's like when things get *really* tight. No movies. No holidays. No restaurants. No dance classes. No visits to the Science Centre or the Aquarium or the Planetarium. No double-fudge chocolate chip ice-cream cones with sprinkles from that place down at the beach...

No *allowance*!

Next, I felt frustrated. How come the police couldn't find one lousy crook? There must be a clue or two lying around somewhere. In mystery books, there were always at least a *few* clues. Didn't they look? Didn't they care?

Then, all of a sudden, I felt a third feeling. Excitement. It hit me the way that first bite of pizza hits your stomach on a day when you've missed lunch.

I thought about all the mystery books I'd read— must have been hundreds of them. I'm crazy for

mystery stories. I read them every chance I get—
in bed at night after my mom's asleep, in science
and spelling classes where I hide them under my
textbooks. I read them on the bus, in the bathtub,
on the toilet...

I must have learned *something* from all those
mysteries. Was there any reason why I couldn't
solve a mystery that was happening in my
very own house? Was there any reason why I
couldn't at least *try* to catch the real live thief who
was trying to ruin my mother's life? And mine,
too?

None that I could think of.

I grabbed my mom's hand and pulled her up
out of the chair. "Come on," I said. "Let's go look
at the scene of the crime."

"Stephanie..." she said suspiciously as she followed me into the kitchen, "what are you up to?"

"Nothing, Mom," I mumbled. When I saw the
kitchen table, I stopped dead. "Wait a minute. You
said *all* the money was stolen."

"I don't remember saying that. But it doesn't
really matter, does it? There were only these coins
left behind." She picked up a roll of quarters from
the kitchen table. There were eight more rolls, all
lying neatly side by side on the table.

"Mom, these are quarters! And loonies! They
must be worth a bundle!"

"Maybe a hundred dollars or so." She shrugged,
as if a hundred dollars were nothing. "But the thief
got away with over nine hundred. The thing I can't
figure out is how someone got into the house. I'm
absolutely *sure* I locked both doors. I checked the

14

windows, too. And the only people who have keys are you and me."

She turned and frowned at me. "You haven't given your key to anyone, have you, Steph? Or lost it?"

"No," I said quickly, but that got me thinking. Something started poking away at the edges of my memory. I waited for it to work its way in.

"Gertie Wiggins!" I said, snapping my fingers.

"What?"

"Gertie Wiggins has a master key. She can get into any town house or apartment in the whole co-op. Don't you remember? She let us in that day we both locked our keys inside the house."

"Oh, gosh." My mom's eyes were suddenly huge. "You *don't* think poor old Gertie could have done this?"

I stopped to think about it. Gertie's a strange one, all right. Short and kind of pear-shaped, with a skinny top end and a fat bottom. Her hair is red and fuzzy, and she wears orange lipstick and green eye shadow and tons of purple-pink stuff on her cheeks. Mostly, I had noticed her out gardening in the courtyard, always muttering away to herself in an annoyed voice, as if she were arguing with someone. Sometimes she sings songs with no words — just la-la-la in this odd husky voice. Some of the little kids in the co-op call her Crazy Gertie.

"Gertie is — well — odd," said my mom. "But I can't believe she would do something like this."

My mom's like that. She has a hard time believing anything nasty about anyone. But if there's one thing I've learned from mystery books, it's this: a detective has to stay open to all possibilities.

Then I remembered something else. I opened my mouth to tell my mom and then shut it again. No. She was worried enough. What I remembered was this: early that morning, as I ran out the door to go to school, I had seen Gertie Wiggins hanging around in the courtyard. She had a spade in one hand and a rake in the other, as if she were gardening. But looking back, through the eyes of a detective, I could see that she was definitely lurking. Suspiciously.

"Well," said my mom, "this is getting us nowhere." She stood up briskly, looking almost normal. Only her red nose showed how upset she had been. "It's almost four-thirty, Steph. If you get started right now, you'll have time to clean your room before dinner."

"My room!" I said. "Are you kidding? What about the robbery?"

"What about it? If the police can't help, then there's nothing we can do. I'll just have to tell everyone what happened, and if—and if—" Suddenly, her courage disappeared again. Her chin started to quiver like it was on a hinge.

"Listen, Mom," I said quickly, "I've read tons of mystery novels, you know, and lots of them have robberies, and I—"

My mom shook her head. "Stephanie, this isn't a game. This is serious business. *Adult* business."

"Mom, will you take a good look at me? I'm almost as tall as you are."

She looked at me. Then she pinched my cheek.

I *hate* it when she does that. "Tall or not, you're still a child. And you've got the messiest room in all of Vancouver. Now scoot!"

I stomped down the hall to my bedroom. Scoot yourself, I thought! Didn't she know that when you're eleven and a half years old—*practically* a teenager—the most horrible words in the entire English language are "You're still a child"? And how could she think about messy rooms at a time like this? I kicked a stuffed puppy and an old headless Barbie out of my doorway to get in.

So, okay. So maybe my room *was* a bit messy. So maybe there *was* a mountain of dirty clothes— also some games and shoes and books and stuff— in the middle of the floor. There were more important things to think about—such as how to catch a thief!

I climbed over the pile of stuff on the floor and headed for the bookcase. The top shelf was full of mysteries, and I pulled a bunch out. Nancy Drew, the Hardy Boys, Encyclopedia Brown. Even a couple of adult mysteries that I'd bought at garage sales. The detectives in these were Hercule Poirot, a bald little guy with a huge moustache, and Miss Marple, a clever old lady. These stories were harder to understand, but worth it, because someone always got murdered. I glanced through a few, looking for tips.

Trouble was, I didn't *feel* much like a detective. Maybe it was because of what my mom had said, but the more I looked through the books, the more I felt like...like a kid! I glanced into the full-length mirror beside the bookcase. Looking back was this long skinny girl with wild, curly brown hair. She had a pointy freckled nose and a wide mouth that was sagging in a pout. She was wearing pink jeans and a pink T-shirt with a picture of planet earth on the front.

Did this girl look like a detective? Definitely not.

And Stephanie! What kind of name was *that* for a detective? Stephanie's a name for a cute little girl in patent-leather shoes and a ruffly dress. The kind of little girl I had been six or seven years ago—the kind of little girl my mom still thought I was.

I slumped down, discouraged, and started putting the books back on the shelf. That's when the comic book fell out onto the floor. It must have been stuffed between a couple of books.

Well, guess who? Superman! Zooming across the sky, a huge red S across his chest, his cape spread wide in the wind.

I looked at him; he looked at me. Slowly, a grin spread across my face. Why? Because I knew he wasn't *always* Superman. Sometimes he was Clark Kent—a nerdy guy in glasses and a suit who worked for a newspaper. When he wanted to be Superman, he had to change into his Superman outfit.

I stood up and headed for my closet.

On the closet floor was another pile of clothes, a lot like the one in the middle of the room. After shuffling through it, I found what I was looking for. I whipped off the pink jeans and T-shirt and changed into my new outfit. Then I headed back to the mirror.

But wait! What about my name? Somewhere in my desk . . . I ran over and started poking around in the top drawer. Old glue bottles, broken pens, empty potato-chip bags—yes, here it was. A roll of labels that said "HELLO, MY NAME IS" at the top. I grabbed a felt pen and printed in big red letters on one of them, "S. O. DIAMOND, DETECTIVE." I looked at the label. Not bad. But then I tried saying it.

No way. I sounded like a gas station. I crumpled the label up and threw it in the garbage.

I tried again. On a second label, I printed "STEPH DIAMOND, DETECTIVE." Steph is what my mom and dad call me for short. I looked at the label. Steph was awfully close to Stiff. In mystery books, a stiff is a corpse. One thing I did *not* want to be was a stiff. Into the garbage!

Okay now, I told myself. Think. I stared at the third label. It lay there blankly. When the name finally came to me, I almost yelped. I printed it quickly and said it out loud.

Yes, yes, *yes*! Perfect. For a moment, I just stood there and let the taste of my new name spread through my mouth. Then I pulled the backing off and smacked the label onto my chest. I crossed the room and stared into the mirror again.

Staring back was a long thin girl with wild, curly brown hair and a pointy freckled nose. She was wearing black tights (easy to run in and invisible in the dark), a long-sleeved black T-shirt (dead plain and serious, with nothing written or drawn on it), black socks, and black baseball shoes with only a thin rim of red around the edge. She looked lean and strong and smart. I knew who she was. I could read it on the label. She was:

STEVIE DIAMOND, DETECTIVE

And she already knew what her first job was. Before the night was through, she was somehow going to get herself inside the apartment of Gertie Wiggins. Crazy old lady. Gardener.

And maybe . . . thief!

CHAPTER

I RUSHED THROUGH DINNER AND HOMEWORK, BUT even so, it was getting dark by the time I was ready to start detecting. The first thing I needed was an excuse to get out of the house. Fortunately, there was that mountain of dirty clothes on my bedroom floor.

"Okay if I take this stuff over to the laundry room?" I asked, staggering into the living room under a huge pile of pants and shirts and socks.

"Help!" cried my mom. "I'm going to faint! Stephanie Diamond is actually doing her *own* laundry."

"Cut it out, Mom. I'm not that bad."

"No, you're not," she said, as she got up off the couch. "In fact, you're terrific. You're so terrific that I'm going to let you do a few of my things, too. Wait while I get the basket."

So then I had to hang around while she sorted through her dirty clothes. Detectives in books never have to put up with this kind of stuff.

"Don't forget," she called out as I left. "The delicate cycle for my colours! And use borax with the whites!"

"Okay, okay," I mumbled.

It had gotten windier over dinner, and my hair whipped around my face as I crossed the courtyard. I had to keep grabbing at pieces of laundry to keep them from flying away. Luckily, the wind was blowing in the direction of the main building, where the laundry room is—also, where Gertie Wiggins lives. In Khahtsahlano Housing Co-op, families live in town houses like ours. Single people live in the apartment building, which is separated from the town houses by the courtyard. I knew that Gertie Wiggins lived on the third floor of the main building.

The courtyard was even worse than usual that night. I had only lived in the co-op for five weeks, but every night of those five weeks, the courtyard had been a mess—always littered with garbage that blew over from the Fabulous Red Burger Barn.

The Red Barn is a fast-food restaurant across the back lane from the co-op. It has this gimmick to bring in customers, especially kid customers. It sells its burgers in large plastic animals and gives them these names that I *personally* think are dumb, but you can judge for yourself. A regular burger—made out of beef—is a Moo Burger. It comes in a big plastic cow about the size of a shoe box, with this silly smile on its face. A chicken burger is called a Cluck Burger and comes in a plastic chicken. And a bacon burger? You guessed it—an Oink Burger—and it comes in a pig.

See what I mean? Dumb.

It was kind of strange for my mom and me to end up living so close to the Red Barn. About six months ago, Garbage Busters had picked it as the worst over-packager in the whole city. They launched this big campaign to try to get the Red Barn people to change to real plates, instead of using throw-away plastic packages. They wrote a bunch of letters and collected names on petitions, stuff like that. They demonstrated in front of the restaurant, too, and talked to customers. But so far, no luck at all. The Red Barn hadn't changed a thing.

You could tell just by looking around our courtyard. There was always some Red Barn garbage around, but on this evening, with the wind, things had gotten really out of hand. Plastic pigs caught in the bushes, plastic cows littering the playground area, plastic chickens blown up against the side of the apartment building. Paper napkins, too, covered in red and yellow smears of ketchup and mustard. One of them was caught between the spokes of my bike—severely gross— but I was in too much of a hurry to stop.

The laundry room was empty. Thank goodness. I dumped the dirty clothes on the floor in the corner, crossing my fingers that no one would figure out they were ours and report back to my mom. Then I dashed down the hall to the elevator and pressed the button. That's when I realized— I didn't have a clue what to do next.

I could, of course, just knock on Gertie Wiggins' door and ask her straight out about her whereabouts that morning and about her master key. But something told me that Gertie Wiggins wasn't going to be thrilled at the idea of answering my questions. Or, I could find some other excuse to get inside her place to look around. Like trying to sell her some Girl Guide cookies maybe. But where was I going to get Girl Guide cookies at that time of night?

Besides, she was crazy. I reminded myself of this fact as the elevator door opened on the third floor.

"Aaaaghh!"

My yell scared even me. Couldn't help it. You'd yell, too, if you were nearly knocked off your feet by a giant. It was Arnie Sykes. He was wearing a pair of ripped jeans and a stained T-shirt that said "Boogie Till You Puke."

"Hunhh!" he grunted as he pushed past me into the elevator. Arnie is this absolutely *huge* guy who lives on the third floor. Must be six foot six and weighs probably half a ton. He's an adult, but not a very old one — only twenty or twenty-five. His hair is long and black, and he combs it behind his ears in greasy curls so that you can see the ten or so earrings he wears in his left ear.

"Why don't you look where you're going?" I muttered under my breath. I wanted to say it out loud, but Arnie's not the kind of guy you start arguments with. The elevator door closed behind me without a word from Arnie. He didn't even grunt.

Then, down at the far end of the hall, I heard the sound of a door opening. Jumping backwards, I banged into another door. The stairs! Pushing the door open, I slipped into the stairwell.

I recognized the squawking noise immediately.

Gertie Wiggins always drags her laundry around in this little two-wheeled shopping cart that's easily a hundred years old. It needs oil badly, and you can hear it coming two floors away. It was headed for the elevator.

I waited until I heard the elevator come and go. Then I snuck back into the hallway and crept quickly along till I came to number 308—Gertie's apartment.

I turned the knob. Must have had beginner detective's luck because the door opened and there I was—in Crazy Gertie's living room.

At least, I think it was her living room. Hard to say, because there was no couch. Only a couple of old easy chairs, one lopsided and made out of fuzzy brown stuff and the other covered in red plaid material that had been patched up a few times. No TV either. Only an old plastic radio, like you see in junk stores. It was on top of a bookcase made out of bricks and boards and filled with tattered-looking books. In the far corner was an old china cabinet with cracked glass doors. The furniture was pretty crummy, but I wouldn't have noticed that much—our furniture is pretty crummy, too.

No, the thing that made the room different was the plants. It was like a jungle in there. They crept along the top of the bookshelf and the radio and the china cabinet. They trailed out of huge pots hanging by thick ropes from the ceiling. And the floor was covered with them. As I stepped into the room, the creeping vines seemed to reach right up and grab at my legs.

"SCRAAUUUKKK!!"

The sound, coming from behind me, made me spring into the air like a rubber ball. I hit the ground in a crouch and whirled around, kicking a large ivy plant right out of its pot.

A giant cockatoo was giving me the evil eye. It had been sitting quietly in a corner behind a huge rubber tree, watching me, all along.

"SCRAAUUUKKK!" it said again, staring at me out of nasty little birdy eyes.

"Scraauukk yourself!" I said, rubbing my toe where it had hit the plant. "Look what you made me do."

Dirt was scattered all over the floor. I picked up the plant as carefully as I could and dropped it back into the pot. The dirt could stay where it was. Gertie Wiggins was not going to spend her whole evening hanging around the laundry room. I had to move fast.

Starting with the bookshelf, I snooped around and checked for things stuck between the books. I wasn't sure what I was looking for, but I figured I'd recognize it if I saw it. What I really hoped to find was stacks of fives and tens and twos, wrapped in elastic bands.

Gertie Wiggins had a big collection of gardening books. Also a lot of plays, including the complete works of William Shakespeare. There were some mysteries, too. *Death on the High Slopes. Murder Most Foul. Scream in the Night.* They sounded great. I pulled out *Scream in the Night* and started leafing through it, wondering whether Gertie might be willing to lend her books out to neighbours.

Then I remembered why I was there. "Cut it out, Stevie," I told myself firmly, shoving *Scream in the Night* back into the row of books. "Concentrate!"

An ugly thought came to me. Maybe other people didn't read mysteries the same way that I did. Cheering for the detective, I mean, and trying to solve the crime. Maybe some people took the side of the criminal. Maybe some people studied mystery stories to learn how to *commit* crimes! The thought gave me the shivers. I remembered the locked door of our town house and Gertie's master key.

Quickly I moved on to the china cabinet. The first thing I saw made my stomach do a little flip — the kind of flip that warns you that you're about to throw up. It was a huge knife. A dagger, I suppose. It had a shiny curved blade that was at least eight inches long. It was *not* the kind of knife you'd use for slicing bread. Right beside it was a small revolver. A gun! In a china cabinet! What kind of old lady was this Gertie Wiggins anyway?

On the next shelf down were more ordinary objects — a silver candlestick, a vase and some fancy little teaspoons. The bottom shelf got weird again. There was a whole collection of tiny coloured pots and a box full of greasy-looking sticks. One of the little pots had a label. It was spotted and faded, like it was really old. I crouched down to have a closer look at the tiny cramped letters:

BLOOD

Okay, I thought. Take it easy, Stevie. Don't

panic, don't get excited. I closed my eyes, then opened them again.

Yup, still there. And right beside it was something else—something round and white, with a big spot on it.

No! It wasn't!

Yes. It was.

An *eyeball*!

That's when I heard it. Screeeeck, scraawwk. Not the cockatoo. The sound was definitely coming from the hallway. The laundry cart!

I admit it. I panicked. For a minute I just stood there, frozen in front of the china cabinet. Then I raced for the door. It wasn't until I had my hand on the knob that I realized—Gertie was just on the other side! I was trapped!

Jerking my hand back, I glanced frantically around the room. Nowhere, absolutely nowhere to hide a full-sized, almost-twelve-year-old girl. The squawking in the hall was getting louder. Closer. Then it was joined by squawking in the living room. My dash across the room had made the cockatoo go berserk. It was shrieking and cawing and flapping its wings at me.

I could hear Gertie's husky voice in the hallway—just behind the door. "It's all right now, Freddy. I'm coming, I'm coming."

No time to think. I charged through the first open door. Against the far wall, I could dimly make out a single bed. It was covered by a patchwork quilt that hung almost to the floor. Not perfect, but it would do. I dived under the bed just as the apartment door slammed shut. The bed was fairly high off the floor, as beds go. Still, I barely fit. I pushed and squeezed and wriggled myself all the way under. As I pulled my feet in behind me, I managed to whack my big toe—the same toe that I'd kicked the plant with—against a leg of the bed. I bit my lip hard, so I wouldn't yell.

"You hush now, Freddy, hush. Mommy's home. You stop that racket now. What's gotten into you?" Gertie's voice from the living room.

The cockatoo quieted down, and I could hear the laundry cart again. Then, suddenly, the space where I was hiding lit up. Gertie must have turned on a light.

From where I was lying, I could see the cart wheels come slowly into view, followed by two large feet in men's leather bedroom slippers. The wheels and the feet stopped right in front of me. I could have reached out and touched them. There was a pause—I tried not to breathe—and a few grunts. Gertie, I realized, was taking her laundry out of the cart. The feet moved across the room, headed for the closet.

Suddenly they stopped. I heard a sharp gasp and saw the feet shuffle quickly back into the living room. They stopped beside the plant I had knocked over. I could even see the dirt, still scattered across the rug. The feet disappeared again. I could hear them padding rapidly around the apartment. Doors opened and shut. The cockatoo started squawking again. And then, silence—except for my heart, which was banging away like a loose shutter on a haunted house.

The feet! They were back. Right in front of me, facing the bed. I closed my eyes, I held my breath. I could almost feel Crazy Gertie's hands on my shoulders, hauling me out.

Nothing. Just silence.

When I couldn't stand it any more, I opened my eyes. The feet were still there. I took tiny shallow breaths. Silent breaths, I hoped. I hoped, too, that Gertie couldn't hear my heart pounding.

"Socks," she said in a strange soft voice. "Always losing socks. Blue socks, red socks, sock 'em in the eye, soccer players, soccerooo..." Her voice got sort of singsong then and died away. I could tell by the rustling sounds that she was back to folding laundry.

It seemed to take forever, but finally the laundry cart squawked its way into a closet, and Gertie disappeared. I'll make a run for it, I thought, and grabbed a bed leg to haul myself out. But then, more shuffling and Gertie's voice again, low and spooky, singing to herself. I froze. The feet again! Bare this time and almost covered by a long flannel nightgown.

"Sometimes I have a great notion," sang Gertie in that same creepy voice, "to jump into the river...and drown..."

Without any warning, she turned out the light and collapsed on top of the bed. I couldn't *see* her collapse on top of it, of course. But the way the bottom of the bed came down on my back gave me the general idea. It pushed all the air out of my lungs with an "Ouff!" that I barely managed to keep silent.

Trapped! Squished so flat I could hardly breathe. Who could believe that one little old pear-shaped lady could be so heavy? She was wriggling around up there. Getting comfortable, I supposed. Then she turned on a dim light beside her bed, and I heard pages turning.

Great, I thought. Just terrific! She was going to start *reading*. Maybe she was like me and read till two or three in the morning. Maybe I'd have to spend the entire *night* squashed like a bug under Gertie Wiggins' bed.

I thought about my mom. She'd be wondering about me by now. She might even be in the laundry room, looking for me. When she saw our clothes — still dirty — in the corner, and me gone, she'd flip right out. She'd figure I got sucked down a machine or something.

That's when I remembered. *The Case of the Kidnapped Carmichaels.* One of the kids escapes by crawling on his belly across the half-dark room where the kidnappers are. With just the bedside light on now, Gertie's bedroom was almost dark. And I was wearing my all-black detective outfit. If I could get out from under the bed, maybe I could slither along the wall until I reached the bedroom door. Then I could bolt for it. I knew I could outrun Gertie easily, and she'd never even know who had snuck in. More important, she wouldn't be able to tell my mom.

By stretching my arms out in front of me, I was able to grab hold of the two bed legs at the foot of the bed. I pulled as hard as I could and was pleased to feel myself move forward a few inches.

I did it again. Above me, Gertie was laughing—at something in her book, I guessed. Good! I blew a dust ball out of my face and crept forward. It was slow going, with all that weight on top of me, but after five or ten minutes, I finally got my backside free.

After that, it was easy.

I was slithering along the far wall, slowly and carefully—trying my very best to look like a spider—when a voice as rough as sandpaper stopped me short.

"Hold it right there, Buster," said Gertie Wiggins, as she rose from her bed. "You're not going anywhere."

CHAPTER

BUSTER? SHE CALLED ME *BUSTER*? I'M NOT EXACTLY what you'd call sweet and dainty. But I'm certainly not a Buster.

Maybe it was the dust balls. I stood up and brushed them out of my hair and off my T-shirt and tights, which were streaked with grey.

"Uh...excuse me," I said, wondering how to talk to a crazy person who kept a pot of blood in her china cabinet. "I guess you didn't notice. I'm a girl."

"Whatzat?" Gertie snapped. She was on her feet now, both fists planted firmly on her wide hips. Her nightgown ballooned out like a tent, yellow with pink flowers. Her eyes were all scrunched up like raisins, and her lower jaw stuck out way in front of her face. She was breathing so hard she was practically snorting.

"Well—" I was glad that the dagger was in the china cabinet and out of Gertie's reach. She looked ready to peel me like a potato. "You just called me—uh—Buster."

"I'll call you anything I please, you thieving rat-faced little git!" yelled Gertie Wiggins. "I ought to give you a good whack across your foolish head!"

She took a couple of steps towards me, too, as if she were going to do it. But the sight of her coming at me like that made me remember what had brought me there. Garbage Busters. The robbery. My mom's job.

"We'll just see who the thieving git is," I yelled back, although I had no idea what a git was. "*You're* the thief around here! Where did you put the Garbage Busters' money?"

As soon as I said it, I knew I'd gone too far. If I'd been able to grab a stack of ten-dollar bills and wave it in her face, I would have been on solid ground. As it was, I had nothing—not even one tiny scrap of evidence. Except for the master key, that is. And the way she had lurked around in the courtyard.

Gertie leaped forward faster than you'd imagine an old lady could move. She grabbed me by the upper arm, her bony fingers digging in like crab claws. Before I knew it, I had been dragged out of the bedroom and into the living room and dumped onto the red plaid armchair. At first I thought she was planning to tie me up or something. But instead, she pulled up the furry brown chair and sat down, facing me. Her hair must have gotten messed up while she was lying on the bed. It lay dead flat to her head on one side and stuck out weird and bunchy on the other.

"Okay, bub," she said in a very quiet voice. "I know who you are. You're that Diamond woman's kid. What I want to know now is what you're doing in my apartment and what you mean about this thieving business."

I didn't have much choice. I ended up telling her the whole story—the Garbage Busters' money, my mom crying, the police, the locked door. Everything. She listened. At least, I think she did— it was hard to tell because her eyes would wander off, and once in a while she'd interrupt me by making these strange little clucking noises with her mouth. When I'd finished, she just sat there, saying nothing.

Then she laughed—an unpleasant croaking sound, sort of like a frog with a bad cold. "Of all the half-baked notions," she said, shaking her head. "You came sneaking in here just because I have a master key? Do you think I'm the only person in the whole co-op who has a master key?"

"What? You mean there are more?"

" 'Course, there are more," said Gertie, waving her hand vaguely at the door. "This is a co-op! We all work together to run the place. A whole bunch of us have master keys."

I was stunned. A whole bunch?

"Who?" I asked. "Who has keys?"

Gertie's eyes were wandering again, and she was muttering to herself. Suddenly, she turned and stared right at me. She had this odd expression on her face.

"You wait right here," she said sharply, pointing her finger at me. "Don't you move."

She got out of her chair and, with a final glance back at me, began moving slowly across the room towards —

The china cabinet! The dagger!

I may be reckless. Well, okay, sure, I *am* reckless. One thing I'm *not*, however, is stupid. By the time Gertie reached the china cabinet, I was already halfway through the front door.

"Wait!" she yelled. Her cockatoo screeched, too—a final "Scraauuukkk!" Maybe there was more, but that's all I heard. I was on the stairs, racing down, three steps at a time, my heart beating almost out of my chest.

The wind was fierce as I flew across the darkened courtyard. It was tossing the plastic animals around, flinging them up against the buildings and fences. Something blew in my face. I tried to brush it away, but it clung to my hand like a cobweb. Eww, yuck—a dirty paper napkin from the Red Barn.

I flung it away and ran for our town house. Falling through the door, I sank into the big green chair. I had a stitch in my side, and I was breathing so hard my throat hurt. Never in my entire eleven-and-a-half years had I been so glad to get home. Never.

"Stephanie!"

Uh, oh—my mom's voice, sounding panicky, from the kitchen. She rushed in, hair flying, arms waving around. "Where on *earth* have you been? What have you been doing?"

How was I supposed to answer that? I mean, think about it. I had just escaped from a crazy old lady who was reaching for her eight-inch, razor-sharp dagger. Before that, she had tried to suffocate me under her bed. And before *that*, I had been trampled by a giant, attacked by a plant pot and insulted by a cockatoo. Not to mention being temporarily blinded by a dirty napkin. I hadn't even caught my breath yet.

I was going to have to explain all *this* to my *mother*?

"Where were you?" she repeated.

"Uh, just—you know—hanging out around the co-op." I shrugged.

I won't bore you with the details of the next half hour. It was all the usual stuff: I-was-looking-everywhere and didn't-you-hear-me-call-you and I-was-worried-sick. The good part was that she was so worked up about me being missing, she didn't even ask about the laundry, which was still in a grubby heap on the laundry-room floor. The other good part was, it gave my heart time to slow down. After I'd said yes-Mom-sorry-Mom enough times, maybe ten or twelve, she finally let up.

"I'm just glad to have you back, that's all," she said, squeezing me so tight my bones squished together. "Now brush your teeth and off to bed."

"Yes, Mom."

She kissed me good night and turned to go to her room.

"Uh...Mom?" I tried to ask it as casually as possible. "Do you know who else has a master key to all the town houses and apartments? Besides Gertie Wiggins, I mean."

"What? You mean there are others?"

"Yeah," I said. "I think so."

She looked at me suspiciously. "What are you

up to? This doesn't have anything to do with the robbery, does it?"

"Robbery? What robbery? No, I was just thinking. What if I get locked out of the house sometime? I don't really feel like asking Gertie for her key." That was true enough. "So I was wondering—who *else* has one?"

"Hmmm," my mom said. "I'm not sure, but it's probably somewhere in the Co-op Handbook—the one they gave us when we moved in. Now, let me see. Where did I put that?" She fished around in some file boxes on the counter. After a minute, she pulled out a thick booklet with an orange cover. "Here it is."

"Thanks, Mom. I'll look through it myself."

"Okay," she said, yawning. "Tell me when you find out. I wouldn't mind knowing myself."

Grabbing a pear and a handful of crackers, I headed for my room. I climbed up into the top bunk of my bed and stared—as I do every night—out the window.

I couldn't help it. It was the view. My window looks right out at the Fabulous Red Burger Barn sign. It's probably the neatest sign in all of Vancouver. It's made of neon lights, with this huge egg on it. At least, it starts out as an egg. But then it cracks open, and this chick comes out. And the neon chick grows and grows until it's a full-grown rooster, and then it starts crowing. "Cockadoodle-doo!" Only it's not very loud and sounds more like "*ruh*-ruh-*ruh*-ruh-*rooooo!*" Then it shrinks back to a chick, and finally the egg pieces come up around it, and it's an egg again. Then it starts all over. I love it. It's so corny.

I watched it, half-hypnotized as usual, for about five minutes. Then I remembered the handbook.

Who else had keys? It only took me a couple of minutes to find what I was looking for, on page 16 at the bottom: "Master-key Holders." Four names. A shiver ran through me. Any name on this list was automatically a suspect. Any of these people could have gotten into our town house today. Gertie Wiggins was right at the top of the list, where she belonged. My prime suspect—especially after tonight! But, I reminded myself, a good detective keeps an open mind. I had no evidence against Gertie. Yet.

I pulled out my journal and a red felt pen. On a new page, under the heading "LIST OF SUSPECTS," I wrote in large bold letters the key holders' names:

1. GERTIE WIGGINS
2. HERB CRUM
3. ARNIE SYKES
4. MARCIA KULNIKI

Slowly, I went through the list, starting with Gertie. It gave me the willies to think of my narrow escape from her apartment. Just picturing her china cabinet made the hair stand up on my arms. Beside her name, I wrote "ARMED AND DANGEROUS."

Herb Crum. He's an old man who lives in the apartment building, bald and kind of hunched over. I tried to remember what my mom had said about him: "Poor man. His wife died last year. I don't think he eats very well. Maybe we should invite him over for dinner sometime."

Hmmm...maybe we could do that. Maybe we could invite Herb Crum over for dinner sometime soon. I could slip in a few questions about master keys and watch how he reacted. Beside his name, I wrote "QUESTION OVER DINNER."

I moved down the list. Arnie Sykes. If there was anyone whose name I *didn't* want on my suspect list, it was Arnie. I tried to imagine questioning him. Me looking way, way up till I got a crick in my neck. Him staring way, way down, as if I were a mouse. I shuddered. Maybe being a detective wasn't such a good idea after all. Even if I did get up enough nerve to question Arnie, I'd be lucky to get even a grunt out of him; he wasn't exactly what you'd call chatty. Beside his name, I wrote "SUSPICIOUS CHARACTER."

Finally, there was Marcia Kulniki. I didn't know much about her. Only that she was a single mom and didn't have much money. Aha! A motive. Beside Marcia Kulniki's name, I wrote "BROKE, NEEDS CASH."

Then I remembered Jesse. He's her son, same age as me—a nerdy little guy who wears a Toronto Blue Jays baseball cap. Jesse's pale and skinny and on the runty side—except for his feet, which are probably a man's size 12. He trips over them when he walks. Or maybe he just trips over his shoelaces, which are always undone and dragging behind him.

Wait a minute. If Jesse's mom had a master key, Jesse could probably get his hands on it any time he wanted. *He* was a suspect, too! I added his

40

name to the bottom of my list.

"Meowrrr?"

The sound was coming from the floor beside my bed. Radical was looking up at me with his best sweet-and-cute-cat expression.

"Mrrroww?" he asked, pawing at the ladder. Radical has the bottom bunk all to himself, and that's usually how he likes it—he's kind of a loner. Sometimes, though, he feels like having a sleepover.

"Sure," I said, jumping down to get him. Radical is an extremely clever cat, but even *he* can't climb ladders.

When he was curled up at the foot of my bed, I reached over to give him a scratch. "Lazy old cat," I said. "You were here today when the money was stolen, weren't you? Why didn't you bite the thief? Or scratch him?"

He gave me this look. *You must be kidding*, it said. Then he closed his eyes and began to purr.

"Boy, I wish you could talk," I said. "You saw *everything*. You're probably the only creature in the whole world who could identify the thief. If only you could read, you could point a paw at one of the names on my list and—"

Radical stuck his head under the covers.

"Okay, okay," I said. "I'll shut up."

Just before I turned out the light, I took a last look at my list. It looked very professional. But Jesse's name, hanging alone at the bottom, seemed to need something more. I thought about him for a minute—his straggly shoelaces, his goofy baseball cap, his sloppy walk. I added a couple of words. My final, completed list looked like this:

LIST OF SUSPECTS
1. GERTIE WIGGINS — ARMED AND DANGEROUS
2. HERB CRUM — QUESTION OVER DINNER
3. ARNIE SYKES — SUSPICIOUS CHARACTER
4. MARCIA KULNIKI — BROKE, NEEDS CASH
5. JESSE KULNIKI — SERIOUSLY WEIRD

"Good night, Radical," I said. "It's been a long, rough day, but I think I've made progress."

"Mrrrrr," said Radical. It could have meant *Absolutely*! On the other hand, it could have meant *Hah*! I decided to take it as a compliment.

"Thank you," I said, turning out the light.

As I tried to fall asleep, Gertie's apartment kept creeping into my mind. I tried to shut it out, but I couldn't — the bird squawks, Gertie's laundry cart, the dust under her bed — it all came back. And the unexplained mysteries: the funny pots, the gun, the greasy sticks, the dagger.

Worst of all was the eyeball. And the blood. Why would anyone in her right mind — or even her wrong mind — keep an eyeball and a pot of blood in her china cabinet?

It was enough to give a girl nightmares.

CHAPTER

I WAS ASLEEP — DEEP IN A DARK DREAM. SOMETHING had gone wrong with the sign at the Fabulous Red Burger Barn. The baby chick was trying to get out of the egg, but it was trapped. The egg wouldn't break open. I could hear the chick inside, trying to escape.

What was strange was the sound. The baby chick wasn't going "peep, peep, peep" — it was going "SQUEAK, CLICK! SQUEAK, CLICK! SQUEAK, CLICK!"

I opened my eyes and sat up. The sound wasn't coming from the baby chick. It was coming from our front door. I charged down the ladder of my bed and ran into the hall.

"Mom!" I yelled as I raced past her room.

When I reached the front hall, I stopped and stood dead still in the darkness. I was listening so hard that, for a second, I didn't notice the feeling in my bare feet. When I did, I couldn't help making a face. Ewww!

"Mom!" I yelled again.

My feet were definitely wet. Cold. And squishy. I reached for the light switch.

Garbage. I was standing, up to my ankles, in wet garbage—soggy cornflakes, rotten tomatoes, cold mashed potatoes—it was all over the floor of our front hall. Somebody had pushed it through the mail slot. That was the sound I'd heard. "SQUEAK, CLICK" as the mail slot was pushed open and flapped shut.

Who? And were they still outside the front door?

Taking a deep breath, I reached for the door knob and then—bang!—threw the door open.

Nothing! No one. Just the dark and empty courtyard and the Red Barn animals scattered around.

"What's going on, Steph?" My mom's drowsy voice behind me. "What are you doing up? It's past three a.m."

"Look!" I pointed to the garbage at my feet.

She rubbed her eyes and stared. "Oh, my gosh. Did you drop something?"

"Mom! It wasn't *me*! Somebody shoved this stuff through our door."

"What?" Her eyes opened all the way. She put her hand out and touched the mail slot. It was all dark and icky from where the garbage had come through. "I can't believe it! Who on earth would do such a thing?"

"I don't know," I said. "But I'll bet you two weeks' allowance it's the *same* someone."

"Same? Same as who?"

"Think about it, Mom. Somebody phones in the middle of the night. Somebody steals the Garbage Busters' money. Somebody shoves garbage through our mail slot. It's the same somebody."

I picked something out of a mess of coffee grinds, spaghetti noodles and soggy toast. Wiping it off, I handed it to her. "Take a look at this."

It was a chicken head. Yellow and made out of plastic and about the size of a small plum. The bottom—the neck, that is—was jagged and uneven, as if it had been cut with scissors. Or a knife.

"Is that what...I think it is?" my mom asked.

"Yep," I answered. "It's the head of a Cluck Burger container."

"Oh, dear," she said quietly. "Oh, Stephanie. What do you suppose it means?"

For an intelligent woman, my mom sure has a hard time putting two and two together sometimes. Comes from not reading enough mystery books, I'd say. She reads mostly science fiction.

"It's a warning," I said. "To the Garbage Busters. It's telling you to leave the Red Barn alone. The phone calls, too, and the robbery. They were *all* warnings!"

"Oh, no." My mom's hand came up to her mouth. "Oh, that's awful."

"Face it, Mom," I said. "The chicken heads in the garbage mean 'Lay off!'"

My mom straightened her shoulders. She looked pale and serious.

"If you're right," she said, "and someone is trying to warn us not to demonstrate against the Fabulous Red Burger Barn, well, it's not going to work. We are not going to be intimidated. We are not..."

Her voice trailed away. She stared into the empty courtyard. "Did you—see anyone?" she asked nervously.

"No." The skin on the back of my neck was all prickly. "They were already gone by the time I got here."

"Oh," she said. "Well, good." She shut the door quickly and locked it. "There," she said firmly. Then she looked down. "Ugh! What a mess. Go to bed, sweetie, I'll clean it up."

Funny, when my mom tells me to clean up, I never want to do it. But when she offers to do it herself, I always get this overwhelming urge to help her. *You* figure it out.

"I'll get the mop," I said.

We found two more plastic chicken heads in the pile. After my mom went back to bed, I took all three into the bathroom, washed them under the tap and dried them carefully. I cleared a space on top of my dresser and lined them up in a row.

They stared back at me with dumb little birdy eyes.

Believe me, if I could have had my *choice* of clues, I would not have picked three plastic chicken heads. I would have chosen a wine glass with a lipstick smear maybe, or a shred of silk clothing, or a smashed watch with the time stopped. Something dignified and elegant. But no—I got chicken heads. One of them toppled over sideways, looking dumber than ever. I straightened it out before heading back to my bunk.

Radical was right where I'd left him—sound asleep, with his head buried under the covers. "Boy!" I said. "Some guard cat you are!"

I turned off my lamp, but it was hard to calm down, so I watched the sign for a while. Egg to chick to rooster. Rooster to chick to egg. Egg to chick to rooster. I don't know how long I watched before I finally fell into a light sleep—very light. For the rest of the night, whenever I heard a siren or a loud truck passing, I'd be startled half-awake. Nervous. As if I were expecting something.

When I dreamed, it was of huge plastic chickens, clucking angrily in the courtyard outside my window. I could almost see them, pushing and shoving, pressing their ugly plastic beaks against the glass.

CHAPTER

I WOKE UP THE NEXT DAY EAGER TO GET ON WITH detecting. My first day (and night) had had some rough spots, but already I had a list of five obvious suspects. How long could it take to shrink it down to one? Especially now that I had three valuable — if incredibly stupid-looking — clues. I couldn't wait to get started.

But by eight-thirty, I already knew. Things weren't going to work out the way I'd planned.

Take breakfast, for example. My mom was still upset by the garbage shoved through our front door, and she burned the last two pieces of raisin toast. I had to have shredded wheat instead. I *hate* shredded wheat. I especially hate shredded wheat covered in chocolate milk, which was all we had left.

When I headed out the door to go to school, who do you think was waiting? Gertie Wiggins! She was down on her hands and knees under a bush in the courtyard, with all her gardening stuff — spade, rake, fertilizer. As soon as she saw me, she stuck her finger out, pointing right at me—just like last night—and started to get to her feet.

"Hey there!" she shouted. "You!"

Uh, oh. I hadn't spotted the dagger among her gardening tools, but you never knew. I threw a quick wave in her general direction. Then I ran. For a whole block. Without looking back.

In the next block, I hit it lucky. One of the suspects was walking down the street, right ahead of me. Jesse Kulniki. Great! I decided to tail him. I followed him down Broadway and up Fir and down 12th and then up Granville for six blocks. This was exciting. Jesse was heading in the exact opposite direction from Emily Carr School. He was walking fast and looking kind of nervous. It wasn't until he went into an office building that I figured it out. "Leonard Pilcher, Dentist," said the sign. Great! I had tailed Jesse Kulniki to his dental appointment!

Of course, I was late for school. Again. My fourth late in a month. Ms. Wootechuk was *not* pleased. By the time I slid into my desk, I had already missed most of the spider parts she had been talking about. As she explained the rest of them, my mind kept drifting away to the robbery and the garbage-through-the-door. I hardly heard a thing until just before recess, when she said, "Here's your diagram, Stephanie. Please have it completed by Friday."

She handed me this gigantic drawing of a spider with at least thirty different lines sticking out from it. At the top, it said "Please label all parts." I stared at it for a minute. Then I ran my finger over the lines until I found a part I recognized. "HEAD," I wrote.

I put down my pencil and sighed. I was in big trouble.

Coming home after school, I stopped dead in my tracks just outside the co-op. Gertie again! She was standing there talking to—are you ready?—Arnie Sykes! The two of them were cozied up against the apartment building, deep in conversation.

When Gertie saw me, she turned and, just like in the morning, yelled "Hey!" I raced past her, through the courtyard and into my house. When I got inside, I leaned against the door. And waited. For a knock or another "Hey!" But it stayed quiet.

I sat down on the couch and tried to figure it out. I was supposed to be investigating *her.* How come she was—well, it almost looked like she was lying in wait for *me.* Like a stake-out in the movies. And Arnie! What was *he* doing with her? Could the two of them be in cahoots? And why wouldn't they come to my door?

I could think of only one reason: my mom. They wanted to catch me alone, and there was no way for them to know she was still at work.

I was home all alone.

"Boo!"

I must have jumped a foot off the couch. "Mom! Don't *do* that! Do you want to give me a heart attack?"

"Sorry, hon," she said. "I thought you heard me come in. I had trouble concentrating at work, so I thought I'd come home and start dinner early.

You okay?"

"What? Oh, yeah. Yeah, sure."

"Stephanie? Are you sure?"

"Yes, Mother!" I tried not to sound grouchy, but it didn't work. "And would you mind not calling me Stephanie? I've decided to change my name."

"Oh?" she said. "Again?"

"What do you mean—again?"

"Well, don't you remember after you read *Little House in the Big Woods*? You made us call you Laura for almost a month."

"Mom!" I said. "I was six years old."

"And then after you read *Anne of Green Gables*, you insisted that your name was Anne. Anne-with-an-e, you said. And when you—"

"Don't you ever forget anything?" I interrupted. "Anyhow, this is different. This time I'm keeping my new name forever."

"Uh-huh," she said with a smile. "And what's your name now?"

"Stevie."

"Stevie," she repeated. "Not bad. Okay. I'll try to remember. Stevie." But she winked as she said it.

How old do I have to be before my mom takes me seriously? Forty-five?

Over dinner, I worked on getting a dinner invitation for Herb Crum, so I could question him. I wanted to sneak the idea into the conversation so my mom wouldn't get suspicious, but it wasn't easy. As soon as I mentioned Herb's name, she got started on old people and how hard it must be to lose a husband or wife. Then, when I reminded her about what she'd said about Herb Crum's eating habits, she got started on nutrition—how important it was to eat lots of green vegetables and drink water. Then she moved on to my *personal* nutrition, which meant chocolate macaroon cookies and how I ate far too many of them.

"Do you want to end up with teeth like mine?" she asked. "Gold crowns all over the place?"

Eventually, I just blurted it out. "Why don't we invite Herb Crum over for dinner, like you said last week?"

"What a lovely idea," she said. "Of course, we will, hon."

"When?"

"Soon. I promise. Just as soon as things settle down a bit at—at work."

The worried look that flitted across her face reminded me that I'd better get busy. Somewhere out there the thief was still running around loose. My plan was to spend the evening out in the courtyard, doing surveillance. But I had to find a spot where I couldn't be seen. Behind a bush, maybe. And I had to put on my detective outfit.

I was pulling on my socks when my mom knocked on my bedroom door. She looked around with this expression on her face like she'd just seen a dead rat.

"Stevie," she moaned. "Look at this place! I thought I told you yesterday to clean it up."

"What's wrong with it?" I asked. As usual.

"What's wrong with it?" she repeated. "What's *wrong* with it? Just look at all this rubbish." She stepped over the pile in the doorway and picked up a clear plastic bag full of broken seashells. "Garbage everywhere!"

"That's not garbage. That's my stuff. I'm going to use those shells."

"For what?"

"A fish tank, maybe."

"What fish tank? You don't *have* a fish tank."

"Well, no," I admitted. "But you never know. I might get one."

"And what's this old pile of lumber over here?"

"Mom! That's my sculpture. I made it in carpentry class, remember? You told me you loved it."

"Oh," said my mom, staring at it in confusion. "Oh, yes, that's right…what's this? My pantihose! Stevie, what have you done to my pantihose?"

"Relax, Mom. Those are the torn ones you threw out. About a week ago, remember?"

"Oh—oh, yes. So what are they doing here?"

"I rescued them. I thought I might make dolls out of them. You know—those dolls made out of stuffed pantihose with funny old faces sewn on them? I'm recycling. I thought you'd be proud of me."

"Well, I am, honey. I am, but—" She was rooting around in a pile of stuff in the corner of the room. "Grandma Diamond's antique tablecloth!" she cried, dragging out a long white thing. "I've been looking *everywhere* for this."

"Oh," I said, a little nervously. "I was using it."

"What for?"

"For a curtain over my hamster's cage."

"For a *what*?"

"It's old, Mom. What's the big deal?"

Her voice, when it finally came out, was thin and squeaky. "Stevie, it's not old. It's antique! It's been in the family for over a hundred years."

"Well, how am I supposed to know that? It just looked old and junky to me."

By this point, it was clear that my mom was totally rattled. She just stood there, clutching the tablecloth.

"Look, Mom," I said, taking her by the elbow and leading her gently towards the door, "you *know* what happens when you come into my room. You get crazy, right?" I could hear her teeth grinding. "So I have an idea. How about you just stop coming in here? That would solve the problem, wouldn't it?"

She just muttered a bit as she stumbled through the door.

Frankly, I couldn't see the problem. My room looked — well, not perfect...but not bad either. Pretty good, in fact. But maybe that's what happens when you work for an organization called Garbage Busters. Maybe my mom was getting garbage-on-the-brain.

I thought she'd given up, but no such luck. As I tiptoed towards the front door a few minutes later, her voice came clear as a bell from the kitchen. "Stevie Diamond? Is that you? The reason I knocked on your door just now was because I happened to take a peek in the laundry room. Aren't you forgetting something?"

Ouch! The laundry. It had been there all night and all day. I sighed. How was I supposed to fight crime when my whole life was swallowed up in household chores?

"Right, Mom," I called back. "No problem. I was just on my way to do it."

Oh well, I thought, as I poured detergent into the washers, maybe I can still do some surveillance from here. Maybe some of the suspects will pass by the door. Maybe they'll even come into the laundry room. There was a table in the corner, with a big green garbage can full of lint balls and odd socks and empty detergent boxes underneath it. I discovered that, by scrunching myself up as small as possible in the corner behind the garbage can, I'd be invisible to anyone coming in. In between loads, I crawled back there and waited.

And waited.

And waited.

At nine o'clock, I gathered up my laundry and went home.

I might as well have taken a giant eraser and wiped this whole day right out of my life!

In my journal that night, I wrote, "Distinct lack of progress today. Suspects spying on *me*. Need to step up the hunt tomorrow. Find that thief!"

Tomorrow, I remembered, the Garbage Busters were scheduled to demonstrate at the Fabulous Red Burger Barn during the lunch hour. I decided to join them. What I needed, I realized, was to figure out the connection. All my suspects were master-key holders. But the chicken heads in the garbage last night had proved something new — the thief also had something to do with the Red Barn.

The question was this: who on my suspect list had a connection to the Fabulous Red Burger Barn?

CHAPTER

T HE NEXT MORNING AT SCHOOL, MS. WOOTECHUK was still going on about spiders. What they ate, where they lived, how useful they were—even *Charlotte's Web* got worked into the act. Spiders, I thought! How can she drone on about spiders when there are thieves out there, people with pots of blood in their china cabinets, weirdos who shove garbage through your door in the middle of the night?

When the noon-hour bell rang, I ran straight to the Fabulous Red Burger Barn. The Garbage Busters were already there—my mom and about six others—standing underneath the rooster sign. Behind them, the walls of the Red Barn were faded red and a bit chipped in places, like they could do with a coat of paint. Through the plate-glass windows, I could see a few lunch-time customers.

"Stephanie! Hi!" The Garbage Busters' hands were full of leaflets. My mom's best friend, Wilma, and Wilma's boyfriend, Pete, gave me a hug, and the others said nice things about being glad to see me.

"Here, Stevie, take some of these. We're handing

them out to customers as they arrive." My mom gave me a stack of leaflets that said "BOYCOTT THE FABULOUS RED BURGER BARN! MAKE THEM CLEAN UP THEIR ACT!" They said a lot of other things, too, but I didn't have time to read them because customers were coming up to the door.

"Psst!" I said to Wilma, edging up beside her. "What does 'boycott' mean?" Wilma is big and chubby, with long thick hair that's almost white, although her face is still young. She laughs a lot. I like being around her.

"It means don't give them any business," Wilma said. "We're asking people to eat their lunch somewhere else. Someplace that doesn't use so much plastic packaging."

"Excuse me, sir." My mom was talking to a grey-haired man in a leather jacket. "Before you go in there, I wonder if you'd mind reading this." The man took the leaflet and smiled politely. Then he turned and walked straight into the Red Barn.

"Guess it doesn't always work," I said to Wilma.

"No, not always." She grinned cheerfully. "But you'd be surprised how often it does work. Lots of people read the leaflet and leave without going into the Barn."

I took a closer look through one of the windows of the Red Barn. There were people eating lunch, all right—I could see plastic pigs and chickens and cows scattered around the tables—but it wasn't full. Not like it usually is at lunch-time.

"And look over there," said Wilma. "See the TV camera? CQX TV sent a reporter and a cameraman. They're doing a feature on us for the news wrap-up tonight. Terrible publicity for the Red Barn! Just terrible!" She smiled happily.

I recognized the reporter from TV—a pretty woman with dark hair and big eyes. She was holding a microphone in front of two teenaged guys dressed in black jackets and pants. They had leaflets in their hands. Wilma and I edged closer.

"Now that you've read the Garbage Busters' information," said the reporter, "are you going to eat at the Red Barn?"

"Nah," said one of the teenagers, shaking his head. "These guys are right. I don't like this throw-away plastic crap either."

His friend nodded and grinned into the TV camera. "Tell the Barn to buy a few plates!" he said. "Let's go to Benny's Bagels." The two of them laughed and walked away.

"See?" said Wilma. "It's working. It's slow, but it is working. And you know what? It's the kids, and teenagers like those two, who understand. It's the *young people* who are walking away."

Wilma seemed surprised, but I wasn't. Kids know a lot about the environment. It's the adults who are screwing things up.

I wandered closer to the TV camera, in case they wanted a shot of the youngest Garbage Buster. A big mistake. The TV camera was positioned right beside a Red Barn air vent. The smell of frying Cluck Burgers hit me—wham!—like a brick wall.

Heaven, that's what it was. Nose-teasing, breath-stopping—the smell of sizzling chicken brought tears to my eyes. My mouth started watering; my stomach rumbled, growled and snarled. And no wonder! I hadn't eaten a thing since breakfast. I felt like one of those characters in the cartoons—like I could float through the air with my eyes closed, following that incredible smell. I wanted a Cluck Burger sooooooooo bad...

I'd only ever eaten a Cluck Burger once—at a birthday party, when I was nine. It was called a Fabulous Chicken Burger back then, and it came on a plate. My friend's mom was so crazy about the Red Barn's food that she drove us right across town for the party.

I could still remember it—the most delicious, taste-tempting, lip-smacking chicken burger *on the face of the entire earth*! It came covered with—no, dripping with—Fabulous Sauce. Nobody knows exactly what's in Fabulous Sauce, but everybody knows what it tastes like—fabulous!

I leaned closer to the air vent, sucking up the smell. Aaaaaaaaa...

If *only* they didn't use those stupid plastic chickens!

I dragged my nose, and the rest of me, a couple of steps away from the vent and leaned against the building. A plastic chicken blew across my foot. I gave it a kick, sending it spinning across the cement. Then I looked around for my mom.

That's when I saw him. Standing over by the very edge of the Garbage Busters, holding a leaflet—a strange little old man in a green-and-brown checked suit. It was obvious that he was only *pretending* to read the leaflet. What he was really doing was watching the Garbage Busters. He had thick grey hair and a bushy moustache.

His eyebrows were so heavy and dark it looked like a couple of caterpillars were crossing his forehead.

Who was he? Not a Garbage Buster, that's for sure. And not a reporter. A customer? But why was he standing outside?

He turned and stared right at me. I think. Hard to tell through those thick round glasses. When he saw me staring back, he looked startled. I glanced around again and spotted Wilma.

"Wilma? Do you know that—" I pointed and then stopped. He was gone. "There was this funny old man. Right there. He was watching us. He was—"

"Well, hold on to your hat," said Wilma, "because here he comes again."

She was pointing at Herb Crum, who was stomping towards the front door. His mouth was curled down, as if he'd just swallowed five or six lemons, and his round bald head was an angry red. He looked like a bull about to charge.

"No," I said. "Not *that* old man. This was—"

Herb's shouting drowned me out. "—been coming here for thirty years now. All a man wants is a peaceful lunch, and what does he get? A bunch of crazy fools, that's what—meddling where they got no business, trying to spoil things. What's wrong with you people, anyway?"

My mom walked quickly over to him. The TV cameraman focussed in on her and Herb.

"Mr. Crum," she said, holding out her hand. "It's me, Valerie Diamond. Maybe I can explain why—"

"G'wan now," he snarled, ignoring her hand. "Best hamburgers in the city. Been coming here for thirty years. You people won't get away with this, you know. You won't get away with it."

"Mr. Crum—" my mom began again, her hand still held out.

Herb stomped past her, heading for the door. It was heavy, and my mom helped him push it open. He grunted and disappeared.

"What a grouch!" said Wilma. "Do you know that guy, Valerie?"

"Yeah," said my mom, sadly. "It's not his fault. This used to be a fantastic place. An old-fashioned diner where they served the best burgers on the west coast. And now look at it!" She waved at the overflowing trash cans and the coloured plastic animals littering the parking lot.

"They still serve the best burgers," I mumbled. The fabulous smell lingered in my nose.

"Yeah," said my mom. "If only—"

"—they didn't use those stupid plastic chickens!" I finished.

But she had already turned to speak to a woman in a grey trench coat who was coming towards the front door. The woman had reddish-brown hair, cut short, and a thin, bony face. Something about her was familiar. She looked kind of nervous when she saw the protesters and the TV camera, and she pulled her coat closer around her. Keeping her head down, she tried to edge her way through the crowd. But there was my mom, right in front of her.

"Excuse me," said my mom. "I wonder if you'd mind reading—"

The woman looked up and stared at my mom. Now I knew who she was. Marcia Kulniki! Jesse's mother. My mom didn't seem to recognize her. She hadn't met as many co-op people as me.

"Look!" Mrs. Kulniki said to my mom in this sharp half-whisper. "I can't talk to you. Do you understand? I can't talk to you."

I guess the TV reporter noticed how nervous Mrs. Kulniki looked. She hurried over with her microphone and stuck it right in front of Mrs. Kulniki's face. "Belinda Ramji," she said smoothly, "of CQX TV. Can I ask how you feel about—"

"No," hissed Mrs. Kulniki. "No, you can't. Why don't you—why don't you, all of you, just—just—"

At that moment, the door to the Red Barn opened, and a woman in a Red Barn uniform peered out. The badge on her uniform said "Manager."

"Marcia?" she said, speaking to Mrs. Kulniki. "Are these people bothering you? You come on in this way. And you," she said to the TV reporter, "have no right to question our employees."

Employees! I was glad the TV camera wasn't on me just then. It would have showed my mouth dropping open about as wide as the Grand Canyon.

Mrs. Kulniki scooted quickly through the door. I pressed my face against the glass to watch as she took off her coat. Sure enough, she was wearing a Red Barn uniform.

Jesse Kulniki's mother worked at the Fabulous Red Burger Barn. Unbelievable! In just half an hour, I had discovered not one, but *two* connections between my suspect list and the Red Barn. Herb Crum ate there. And Marcia Kulniki worked there. Stevie Diamond, I told myself, you are definitely hot on the trail.

I might have spent the rest of my lunch-hour congratulating myself if my stomach hadn't interrupted. It sounded like a couple of dogs were having a fight behind my belly button. Even Sherlock Holmes, I reminded myself, had to eat. I told my mom and Wilma I was leaving and headed home. I was imagining a homemade sub bursting with ham and cheese, loaded with tomato and lettuce, heavy on the mayo and ketchup, with a couple of slices of pickle on the side.

I was trying to decide whether to put it in a bagel or on an English muffin when I spotted the old man. Not Herb. The funny-looking guy with the weird eyebrows, who had been watching the Garbage Busters. He was standing in the doorway of the apartment building of Khahtsahlano Co-op. I darted behind a tall bush. Pushing the branches aside, I watched as he pulled out a key.

A key? This guy had a key to our apartment building? He stuck it into the lock, opened the door and walked in.

I waited a moment and then followed. It took me a minute to find my key, and I fumbled around a bit, shoving it into the lock. It had gotten a little rusty from being left outside in the rain a couple of times and wouldn't turn at first. When I finally got the door open, the old guy was gone.

Who *was* he, anyway? Where did he go? Maybe I should search the building. I glanced down at my watch.

Rats! It was already ten to one. Barely enough time to run back to school. No time to look for the old man. No time to make a sub either! I ran over to my place and grabbed an apple from the fruit bowl. It wasn't much, but at least I wouldn't starve.

On the way back to school, I discovered that there's one thing worse than a single bruised apple for lunch...

A single bruised apple with a worm hole in it!

"Double rats!" I muttered as I ran in — late again — through the front door of Emily Carr.

Fortunately, it was Library time. I charged into the library and grabbed a book off the shelf. Mr. De Guistini, the librarian, smiled at me as I sat down at a table. He's nice. I smiled back at him and opened my book.

Freddy Duck's Magic Picnic. Great!

Oh well. I was too excited to read anyway. My lunch-hour had turned up some terrific new clues. Not one, but *two* of the people on my suspect list had shown up at the Red Barn and acted very suspiciously. I stared down at the book. Slowly, Freddy Duck's face faded out. It was replaced by Mrs. Kulniki's face, tense and nervous, the way she had looked outside the Red Barn. I closed my eyes and shook my head. Maybe hunger was making me hallucinate.

When I opened my eyes again, Mrs. Kulniki was gone. I was staring instead at Herb Crum's angry scowl—right there, on page 14, in the middle of Freddy Duck's picnic.

As I watched, Herb's face faded. Slowly, a new face appeared on the page. The face of the weird old guy, the one with the eyebrows. I stared at this face for a while as it bobbed up and down on top of the print. Then it stretched out wide, like he was grinning—wider and wider, until I realized what I was looking at.

There it was—the crisp green lettuce, the delicate breaded coating around the chicken, the oozing layer of Fabulous Sauce—warm, fragrant, moist—a Cluck Burger!

Triple rats!

Quadruple rats!

Rats, rats, rats, rats, rats!!!

CHAPTER

"COMPANY FOR DINNER!" MY MOM WAS TIDYING UP the house as I came in. "And *don't* throw your knapsack down on the floor, Stephanie! I'm trying to keep the place clean."

"Stevie!" I yelled, snatching up the knapsack and running for the bread box. Thank goodness! A bag of poppy-seed bagels. Ripping open the plastic, I grabbed two, wolfing the first one down without even moving away from the counter.

"Hungry?" asked my mom.

"Mgmfowf!" I answered, stuffing bagel into my mouth.

When I had eaten enough bagels (three) to keep me alive till dinner, I remembered what my mom had said. Company. Who? Couldn't be Herb Crum. Not after what happened at the Red Barn today.

"Stevie? If you're finished demolishing those bagels, could you get to work on that mess in your room, please? Jonathon will be here in less than an hour."

"Jonathon! Mom! You *didn't*."

"Oh, honey, you're not going to make a fuss, are you?" She shook her head and sighed. "Jonathon was so helpful after the robbery. The least I can do is make him dinner."

"Couldn't you just send him a thank-you note? Or a bunch of flowers?"

My mom gave me one of her don't-argue looks. "Jonathon is my dinner guest tonight. And *you* are going to be extremely polite to him."

"Hmmph!" I said, sticking my lower lip out as far as it would go.

For a moment we just stood there, trying to out-glare each other. Then my mom laughed. "Oh come on, it'll be fun," she said. "And listen—you can decide what's on the menu tonight. Pick anything you like."

"Anything?"

"Anything! Pizza, spaghetti, whatever you like."

"Okay," I said. "I choose the Green Meal."

"Oh, now, Steph—I mean, Stevie...I'm not sure that Jonathon—"

"Mom, you *said* I could choose."

She shrugged. "Okay," she said, after a minute. "I guess Jonathon will have to like it or lump it."

Let me explain the Green Meal. It's sort of a family tradition. We've been making it ever since I read that Dr. Seuss book *Green Eggs and Ham* the year I turned five. As you've probably figured out, everything in it is green. Everything!

This is how you make it. You start by greening up your ham with some green food colouring. Then you crack a bunch of eggs, beat them and throw some green colouring in with them, too.

Then you cook the whole mess up with some butter in a frying pan. That gives you Green Eggs and Ham. But to have a really serious Green Meal, you have to add other green stuff, which is not hard at all, when you think about it. It's amazing how many foods are green.

The thing about the Green Meal is this: I've never met an adult—aside from my mom and dad, that is—who didn't look like they were going to barf at the very sight of it.

Good!

I wandered down to my room and glanced around. Still looked pretty good to me. Instead of tidying up, I found myself remembering all the times Dad and I cooked the Green Meal together.

On top of my dresser—in the place of honour, right behind my rock and shell collections and the three plastic chicken heads—stood a framed picture of my dad. He was standing beside a campfire, an orange tent half hidden in a clump of trees behind him. He had on a pair of baggy jeans and a blue-and-red checked shirt that was half tucked in and half hanging out. His hair was sticking up at the back and looked, as usual, kind of goofy. His nose was on the large side, and his smile was definitely crooked. So were his front teeth. I thought about Jonathon's perfectly handsome looks and shook my head. Poor Dad!

The picture had been taken up in the Yukon, where my dad's doing his research. I wished, for the five hundred and ninety-eighth time, that he could study something in the city. Why did he have to pick mountain goats? Why not pigeons?

Vancouver had plenty of pigeons. Or squirrels. Why couldn't he study squirrels?

I sighed. My dad wasn't interested in pigeons. Or squirrels. I'd tried him on both.

"Stevie!" my mom hollered from the kitchen. "How's that room coming?"

"Fine, Mom," I yelled, picking up a book I'd taken out of the library the week before. *The Clue in the Birthday Cake*. The cover showed two boys and a girl, all ripping apart a huge birthday cake— candles and icing flying all over the place. Great! I opened it up.

Twenty minutes later, I wandered back out to the kitchen. Mom was cracking eggs into a big glass bowl and humming. She was wearing her dangly parrot earrings. *And* perfume.

"Got any ideas for more green things for dinner?" she asked. In her soft purple sweater and her new black pants, she looked great. Almost beautiful.

Rats!

I stuck my head in the fridge. "Frozen peas," I said, trying not to sound grumpy. "Lettuce and celery for salad. And here's some olives. Oh, and avocado. Got any green salad dressing?"

"We'll make some," she said, as the doorbell rang.

It was Jonathon, wearing a pale blue shirt and grey pants and looking like he'd just stepped out of a magazine. I realized that it was the first time

I'd seen him in regular clothes. Jonathon teaches fitness classes part-time, and usually he runs around in these skin-tight, shiny athletic outfits in neon colours.

He handed my mom a bouquet of yellow flowers. "For you, Valerie." His smile showed at least two hundred teeth, all straight and white, like a toothpaste ad. "You look absolutely lovely. What a gorgeous sweater!"

"It's old," I blurted out before I could stop myself. "Really old! She's had it for years. It even has this little hole in the back."

"Stevie!" said my mom. Then she laughed. "Oh, well. Stevie's right, Jonathon. I *have* had it for years. I don't buy many new clothes."

"Good for you!" said Jonathon, nodding his head approvingly. "I like a woman who practises what she preaches. If more people were like you, Valerie, we wouldn't have all this waste and garbage in the world."

This was worse than I thought. He even liked her holey old sweaters!

"And Stephanie, I have something for you, too. A couple of things actually." Jonathon handed me two parcels, wrapped carefully in newspaper, with recycled ribbons around them. All the Garbage Busters wrap their presents that way.

"Gee—uh, thanks, Jonathon." What else could I say? My mom was giving me a look that said *See? He's not so bad, is he?*

The first package contained a lime-green wrist-wallet—one of those little pouches that fasten with Velcro. It was exactly like the one that

Jonathon wore with his athletic outfits.

"Now these are really handy dandy things," he was saying in the kind of bright cheerful voice you hear in TV commercials. "You just wrap them around your wrist, like this, and you can forget about knapsacks. I wear mine all the time. Means I'm always ready to work in a bit of exercise. You never know, do you, when an exercise-opportunity will knock?"

An exercise-opportunity? Was he kidding? No, he wasn't. "Sometimes I jog in place while I'm waiting in a supermarket line." He jogged on the carpet. To show me, I guess.

"Or I might do a few stretches while I'm reading the newspaper." He squatted down and did a few stretches. "It's never too early to develop a proper fitness regime. I could get you started with jogging, if you like."

Jogging? I spend half my life running. "Sure, Jonathon," I said politely. "That would be great."

I looked over at my mom. She was smiling. "I could probably use more exercise myself, Jonathon," she said. "Maybe you could get *me* started jogging."

"Marvelous!" said Jonathon. "We could all jog together. The three of us!" He grinned at us like we were already one big happy jogging family.

This was bad. If they were going to start jogging, I'd have to go along, just to keep them apart. On my list of fun things to do, jogging with my mom and Jonathon came about three hundred and fifty-ninth.

I sighed and put the wrist-wallet on. Maybe it would be useful in my detective work. Maybe I could keep clues in it. Or notes.

I opened the other package. "Wow!" I said. "This is great! This is terrific!"

Peanut brittle. A whole pound of it. For one brief moment, I almost liked Jonathon. Ever since my last dental appointment — four new fillings — my mom had been on the warpath about candy. For a month now, I had been totally deprived.

"Hope I'm not breaking any family rules," Jonathon said, raising his eyebrows at my mom.

"Oh well," she said slowly, "I guess just this once."

"Gee, thanks, Jonathon," I said.

The peanut brittle almost made me feel guilty about making the Green Meal for Jonathon. *Almost*. But then I remembered my dad, how goofy he looked and how far away he was. I looked at Jonathon — at his un-goofy smile and his un-goofy nose and his thick, blond, un-goofy hair.

Time for the Green Meal.

"Dinner will be ready soon, Jonathan," said my mom. "I'm afraid it's a trifle — uh — unusual tonight."

❖ ❖ ❖

Dinner looked lovely. The eggs were a bright slime green, and the ham was almost the colour of rotting leaves. When Jonathon saw it, his face turned the same shade as the avocado, making it just about the greenest meal we'd ever had. After the first shock, though, he tried to be a good sport, digging right in as if he ate green ham every day.

"It *tastes* delicious," he said, trying to smile, "and

it certainly is...uh, creative."

You might not believe this, but I didn't *mean* to spoil Jonathon's wine. All I did was spear my ham, and a pea flew off my plate—totally accidentally! It landed in Jonathon's wineglass. How could I *plan* a thing like that?

"Stephanie!" my mom snapped.

"Sorry," I mumbled.

"Don't worry, Valerie," Jonathon said, removing the pea with two fingers. It left a greasy film on the surface of his wine. "It's nothing. Really. How did the demonstration go today? I felt bad about missing it."

"Don't be silly," said my mom. "It was important for you to follow things up at the police station. I just couldn't face going down there today."

Jonathon reached across the table and put his hand on top of my mother's. "I understand," he said softly. "This has taken a lot out of you, Valerie. I haven't wanted to say anything, but—I've been worried about you." He looked deep into her eyes, like they do in love scenes in the movies.

"Peanut brittle!" I guess it came out louder than I'd planned, because they both jumped. "Who wants some peanut brittle? I'll get it."

When I came back from the kitchen, the two of them were deep in a conversation about Garbage Busters. Usually I don't listen to Garbage Busters stuff, but when I heard my mom say "money," I got interested.

Jonathon was shaking his head slowly and unhappily. "I had a look at the books, Valerie, and it doesn't look good."

"What books?" I said. "What are you talking about?"

"The Garbage Busters' books, honey," my mom said. "The 'books' are the financial records—how much money Garbage Busters has. Is it really bad, Jonathon?"

He took a deep breath. "I'm afraid so. We're overdrawn, and we've got that loan due at the end of the month. The money we collected at Environment Day—the stolen money—would have helped a lot. Of course, those grants might come through in the new year. But for now, well, I'm sorry, but I just don't see how we can manage your salary next month."

He said a bunch more, but the only thing I understood out of it all was "salary." The Garbage Busters couldn't "manage" to pay it. I knew what that meant. Soon my mom would tell me she couldn't "manage" to pay my allowance any more.

"I'm sorry," Jonathon went on, taking my mom's hand again. "You're doing such great work, Valerie. I wish there was a way—"

"It's not your fault, Jonathon." She patted his hand absent-mindedly. "Just bad luck, I guess."

"Well, if there's anything I can do to help—" He leaned closer, staring into her eyes again and dripping handsomeness all over the place.

"Oh, Jonathon, you've been a huge help already. You have no idea—" Now she was staring into *his* eyes.

"Dishes!" I said. Well, okay, I yelled it. They both stared at me like I'd lost my mind. "Time to do the dishes!"

I have to admit that Jonathon was a pretty good dinner guest. He helped carry the dishes into the kitchen and dried after I'd washed them. He even gathered up our newspapers and bottles to take down to the parking garage, where the recycling containers are.

"You don't have to do that, Jonathon," said my mom.

"No trouble at all," he said in his chirpy TV-commercial voice. "We've all got to do our part."

"Oh brother," I mumbled, rolling my eyes at my mom. She didn't notice — too busy being grateful, I guess.

I had hoped that Jonathon would go home right after dinner, so I could get on with detecting. The demonstration had blown the case wide open, and I should have been out there spying on my suspects. But he plunked himself down on the couch and stretched out his legs like he was ready to move in forever. I sighed and plunked myself down on a chair beside him. It was going to be a long evening.

"Don't you have any homework, Stevie?" my mom asked from the kitchen.

I remembered my spider diagram. Darn! I was going to be in big trouble if I didn't do something about that.

"Nothing important," I called out. I leaned back in my chair and put my feet up on a stool. "Guess I'll just hang around with you guys tonight."

Jonathon didn't leave till ten. As I dragged myself off to bed, I hoped that my dad would one day recognize what an enormous sacrifice I had made to save his marriage. Oh, Stevie, he would say, I don't know how to thank you. You're so thoughtful, you're so clever, you're so —

"Messy! Stephanie Olivia Diamond, you come right back here. Look at this! Peanut brittle crumbs all over the rug."

"Sorry, Mom." I turned in my tracks. "I'll clean it up."

A few minutes later, I was in bed with my suspect list. Beside Mrs. Kulniki's name, I carefully wrote "WORKS AT RED BARN." Beside Herb's name, I wrote "EATS AT RED BARN." At the bottom of the list, I added a whole new suspect.

6. OLD MAN WITH EYEBROWS — WHO IS HE???

I stared at it for a minute, as if the letters on the page could give me a clue. But nothing!

As I turned out the light, a familiar sound crept in through the window. *Ruh*-ruh-*ruh*-ruh-*rooooooo*! I thought about watching the sign for a while, but my eyelids felt sooooo heavy ...

I figure it probably took me two and a half seconds to fall asleep.

CHAPTER

LYING IN BED, SLEEPY AND CONFUSED UNDER MY warm covers, there were only two things I was sure about:

1. The house was black. Middle-of-the-night black.

2. Someone was pushing something through our mail slot.

SQUEAK, CLICK! The sound was like ice water thrown over me. I'd heard it before—the night garbage was shoved through our mail slot!

"Oh no, you don't," I muttered. Not again. Jumping down from my bunk, I raced to the front door. As soon as I flipped on the hall light, I saw it—a note, half-crumpled and covered in streaks of dirt. As I snatched it up, my eyes flew over the big block letters.

LEEVE THE RED BARN ALONE. DONT YOU NO THAT PEEPLE COULD LOOSE THERE JOBS OVER THIS? DONT YOU KARE ABOUT PEEPLE AND THERE JOBS?

Kare? Peeple? Another clue. The thief was a horrible speller.

No time to think about that now. Switching off the light, I carefully opened the front door and peered out into the night. The courtyard was spooky under the dim lighting, the trees and bushes just shadowy shapes. I could feel the hair standing up on my arms as I stepped outside.

Nothing.

Then, in a bush halfway down the courtyard, a slight movement. Or was it my imagination? As I watched, a dark shape shifted and was still again.

The thief!

Okay, I know. It was a stupid thing to do. But I couldn't stop myself. I crept out into the courtyard in my bare feet, sneaking slowly from bush to bush and staying close to the building so I'd be out of the light. I glanced down at my pyjamas. Yellow! They practically glowed in the dark. Who would have guessed that a detective would need black *pyjamas*, too?

The figure moved. Suddenly it was a dark blur, flying across the far side of the courtyard. In one quick leap, it was up and over the fence and out on the front sidewalk. I was right behind, quick as a shot. When I hit the sidewalk, I glanced around. The dark shape was down the block, moving fast.

I knew what I *should* do. Stop, of course. Turn back. Tell my mom.

I took off at a run after the thief, my bare feet smacking against the cold concrete. He was ahead, but I picked up speed quickly. As we hit the next block, the thief stumbled once or twice. I didn't. My feet flew across the pavement. All I could hear was my own ragged breathing. I was gaining on him! A fresh burst of speed. I felt like—no, I *was* a pale yellow bullet! I was closer now. Close enough to see how small he was. A kid! Smaller than me.

Suddenly, he tripped and was down! I didn't even think, I just did it. I jumped him.

"Ooowwww!" he yelled, thrashing around underneath me. "Ouch! Get off! That hurts!"

The voice sounded familiar. I reached out to grab his face, so I could turn it into the street light. Something came off in my hand—a baseball cap.

"Jesse Kulniki!" I yelled. "Is that you?"

"Who wants to know?" said a muffled voice.

"I don't believe it," I muttered. "I just don't believe it."

"Owwww!" he yelled. "Stephanie Diamond! Get off my back. Right this second!"

"Not until you tell," I said, adjusting my knees, which were holding down both his arms. He twisted and jerked around, but he couldn't throw me off.

"Owww! Cut it out. Tell what?"

"Tell me how come you're running around the co-op in the middle of the night. Shoving garbage through people's doors! Leaving nasty notes!"

"What are you talking about? I don't know anything about any dumb garbage. Owwww! Stephanie, my face is rubbing on the cement. It hurts. GET OFF!"

I got off him. Slowly. Hanging on to the back of his sweatshirt.

"We're going to my house," I told him. "To talk."

"Uh-uh," he said, trying to get loose. We

wrestled around on the sidewalk for a minute, and finally he sprang free. "Forget it! Why should I?"

"Because if you don't—" I paused, trying to think of how to finish the sentence.

"What?" he said. Nervously. Good.

"I'm going to wake up your mother. And my mother. And the police! You're in big trouble, Jesse Kulniki." I didn't really mean it about the police, but Jesse didn't know that.

"The police!" he squealed. "No, don't! I'll come, I'll come."

We walked back quickly. When we got to my house, I led him into the kitchen, shut the door and turned on the light.

"Keep your voice down," I hissed, "or my mom really *will* wake up."

Jesse sat down on a kitchen chair, arms crossed, shoulders hunched, staring at the floor. He was wearing a mustard-yellow sweatshirt that said "Quality Auto Transmissions" and a pair of faded green corduroy pants. They rode up his legs so I could see his socks—one white, one striped blue and red. His sneakers were grey and huge— bigger than my dad's, I think—and the laces hung out loose on the floor. His knees were jiggling up and down like they were attached to puppet strings.

"All right," I said. "Where is it? Where's the money?"

"What money?" He looked up, eyebrows crinkled together.

"The Garbage Busters' money," I said. "The $963

81

you stole from this table. Where is it?"

"Nine hundred — I don't know what you're talking about," said Jesse. "I swear." He was sitting up straight now, staring at me in amazement.

"Oh, sure," I said, although I wasn't so sure any more. "And I bet you're going to tell me that it wasn't you who shoved that garbage through our door — with the chicken heads in it."

He looked horrified. "Chicken heads? You mean from dead chickens? I wouldn't even *touch* a dead chicken. Stephanie, I'm a *vegetarian*!"

"Not *real* chicken heads," I said. "Relax! They were plastic."

"Oh," said Jesse, calming down a little. "Still, that's no way to treat a chicken. Or any other bird. People think that just because birds are small and helpless, they can do anything they want to them. People think that birds — "

Oh brother, I thought. A vegetarian *and* a bird lover. Maybe he wasn't the thief after all. "What about the note?" I interrupted. "You *did* shove that note through our door."

"Well, yes." His shoulders slumped again, and he stared at the floor. It was a minute or two before he said anything. "It's my mom. She just started working at the Red Barn. It took her ages to find this job. You don't know how hard it is when your mom's out of work, and she's all depressed, and there's hardly any money for anything."

"No, but I might soon," I said, thinking about the Garbage Busters.

"The manager talked to all the employees

today," Jesse went on, "about how business is slowing down. Because of the demonstrations. And now my mom doesn't even have to go in to work till Saturday. Can't the Garbage Busters find some other restaurant to pick on?"

"They're not picking on the Red Barn, Jesse," I said. "It's the worst restaurant in the whole city for making garbage. And it doesn't even *try* to recycle!"

He looked about ready to cry. "I know. It's pretty gross. But that's not my mom's fault. And do you have to close the whole restaurant down?"

"Of course not," I said, remembering the incredible smell of frying Cluck Burgers. "Nobody wants the Red Barn to close down. The Garbage Busters just want them to change to real plates and knives and forks, that's all."

"But the Red Barn *used* to use real plates," said Jesse. "Back when old Mr. Smithers owned the restaurant. My mom and I used to go there for birthdays, and Mr. Smithers always came out with a cake. I remember the plates they used. White with pictures of vegetables around the rim. Carrots, mostly. But when Mr. Smithers died, his family sold the restaurant. It's the new owner. He's the one who got in all the plastic stuff."

"But why?" I asked.

"To get more customers," said Jesse. "The new owner wants to start a whole huge *chain* of restaurants, right across the country. He figures it could be bigger than McDonald's. Plastic chickens and pigs and cows from coast to coast!"

For a moment we just sat there, imagining

plastic pigs floating in the Great Lakes, plastic chickens blowing across the prairies, plastic cows poking their noses out of the high snows in the Rockies. It was an awesome thought.

"Who is this new owner?" I asked.

He shrugged. "No one knows. Mr. Mysterious, that's what my mom calls him. Never even shows up, except sometimes, in the middle of the night. My mom says she doesn't blame him—not with all the bad publicity the restaurant's been getting."

"The middle of the night? That's pretty weird."

Jesse shrugged again. "All I know is, my mom was told to leave the receipts out one night because the owner was coming by to check them. Late. After the restaurant closed."

"Gosh," I said. "Mr. Mysterious, eh?" I was thinking of the guy with the eyebrows. If anybody was mysterious, he was.

"Actually," said Jesse, "it could be Ms. Mysterious, I guess. Could be a she. Like I said, my mom never met her. Him. Uh, her—whatever! What does it matter?"

"Just wondering," I said. "Wondering if there's a connection."

"Connection with what?"

So then, of course, I had to tell the whole story—the robbery, the phone calls, sneaking into Gertie's. When I got to the part about the stuff in Gertie's china cabinet, his eyes bugged almost out of his head.

"Wow!" he said. "Are you thinking what I'm thinking?"

"What?"

"The dagger and the weird little sticks and the blood and eyeball. Doesn't it make you think of...you know, a witch?"

"A witch?" I said. "What are you talking about, Jesse? We didn't get a spell put on us. We got robbed."

"Well, yeah, I know that," said Jesse. "But still— it could explain how she got in. Maybe she walked through a wall."

"She has a key, remember? She can just stick it in the keyhole. She doesn't *need* to walk through walls."

"Oh," said Jesse. "Oh, right."

"Anyway," I said, "that's not the end of it." I told him about the garbage pushed through our door. When I mentioned the chicken heads, he got all excited.

"Listen, Stephanie—" Jesse said.

"Stevie," I told him. "The name's Stevie."

"Okay," he said. "Stevie. Did you find the rest of the chickens yet?"

"What chickens?"

"The ones that got their heads cut off," he said. He was bouncing around in his chair now, talking really fast. "If the thief cut the heads off three plastic chickens, then the *rest* of the chickens might still be around. Like in the thief's garbage. If you find the rest of the chickens—"

"Wow!" I said. "Jesse, you're right. The chicken bodies! I need to find the chicken *bodies*." I was amazed. There was a brain hidden under that baseball cap.

"Uh...Stevie?" he said. He was still wiggling

around in his chair, but he was looking down at the floor now, too. "I was thinking...this detective business sounds pretty dangerous and—uh—maybe you could use, like, a boy or something."

"A boy?"

"Yeah," he said. "A boy."

"Oh, I get it," I said. "You mean—a boy like you?"

"Well, sure...sure, like me."

"Now why would I need a boy?"

"Well, you know. If things got rough...I could protect you. Or, if you got in trouble, I could rescue you."

"What?" I said. "*You're* going to rescue *me*?"

"Sure," he said, crossing his arms on his chest and smiling. "Girls always need rescuing in the movies. Like, when they faint and stuff. Guys rescue them."

Can you believe it? Can you *believe* it?

"Cripes, Jesse," I said. "Who caught *who* tonight?"

"Oh, that," he said, looking embarrassed. "I tripped! On my shoelace! You never would have caught me otherwise."

"Yes, I would."

"No, you wouldn't."

"Would so."

"Would not."

"Would—" I stopped. Nancy Drew would never get dragged into a silly argument like this. "The point is," I said firmly, "that I do *not* need any rescuing."

"Oh," said Jesse, finally getting the message.

There was a long silence while he thought about it.

Then he shrugged. "So okay, so you don't need rescuing. But we could still be partners, couldn't we? I mean—I figured it out about the chicken bodies, didn't I?"

He had a point there. Besides, being a detective all by yourself can get a bit lonely. Maybe a partner wasn't such a bad idea. Of course, if I'd had a choice, I would have picked somebody a bit cuter. Like Mark Heideger, for instance, who is in my class and has the greatest dimples in the entire universe. Or Dylan Wright, who is Mark's best friend and about as cute as you can possibly get without dimples.

But—let's face it—Mark and Dylan weren't in my kitchen, figuring it out about the chicken bodies. Jesse was. And there was something about him—that dumb baseball cap maybe, or the way he got all excited about everything—that made me trust him. "Let me think about it," I said.

He nodded. Then he just sat there, waiting silently—except for his right foot, which tapped away crazily like it wasn't even attached to him.

"Okay," I said. "I've thought about it long enough. You're in. But no rescuing! Got it?" I held out my hand.

"Wow!" Jesse yelled, jerking my hand up and down. "Partners! Oh, Stevie, this is great. This is— wow! Stevie, I—"

"Shhh—" I told him. "You're going to wake up my mom."

"Oh, yeah," he whispered. "Sorry." But he

couldn't stop grinning, and he was on his feet now, bouncing around my chair. "Wow!" he said. "A real crime—"

"Jesse," I said. "If you're going to be my partner, you're going to have to stop being so—so jumpy."

"I'm not jumpy," he said, looking offended. "I'm high-strung."

"Whatever," I said. "Anyway, you better go now. I'll meet you tomorrow after school, and we'll start searching."

"Great," he said. "Where?"

"Where do you think? The garbage."

"You mean, the co-op garbage?"

I nodded.

"Pee-yew. Gross!" he said. "Four o'clock okay?"

I nodded again. He was at the door when I remembered something.

"Jesse?"

"Yeah?"

"Do you get to eat a whole lot of Cluck Burgers? I mean, with your mom working at the Red Barn and all?"

"Well, I could, I guess. Except that I'm a vegetarian. I don't believe in consuming dead flesh." He made a face as he said it.

"Who said anything about dead flesh?" I said. "I'm talking about chicken burgers!"

He shrugged. "I only eat the Red Barn's Veggie Burgers."

"Are they the ones that come in a big plastic tomato?" I had seen a few tomatoes around the courtyard. Obviously, the Barn didn't sell as many of these as the meat burgers.

"Yeah," he said. "I feel bad the vegetables had to die. But I have to eat *something*."

Oh brother, I thought. What I said was, "I guess you couldn't get me a Cluck Burger, could you? I mean, without the package?"

"I don't see how. They stick them in those plastic chickens the second they come off the grill."

"Oh."

I must have looked really disappointed. "I could try," he said.

"Could you?"

"Sure," he said. "Be glad to...partner!" He waved and disappeared.

I wandered back to my bedroom, wide awake. Detecting sure got in the way of a girl's sleep. As I got into bed, Radical stretched and stared at me. I could tell what he was thinking.

"Yes," I told him. "As a matter of fact, I *do* have to leap out of bed every night and run around like a crazy person."

Turning on my bed light, I reached under the pillow and pulled out my pen and list of suspects. A few minutes later, the list looked like this:

1. GERTIE WIGGINS — ARMED AND DANGEROUS
2. HERB CRUM — QUESTION OVER DINNER
           — EATS AT RED BARN
3. ARNIE SYKES — SUSPICIOUS CHARACTER
4. MARCIA KULNIKI — BROKE, NEEDS CASH
           — WORKS AT RED BARN
5. JESSE KULNIKI — PARTNER!!
6. OLD MAN WITH EYEBROWS — WHO IS HE???

I felt a bit funny about leaving Jesse's mother on the list. But I still didn't know anything about her. Except that she worked at the Red Barn and looked nervous.

I added two questions to the bottom of the list. The answers, I figured, would bring me — I mean us, Jesse and me — a lot closer to solving the mystery. They might even lead us to the thief. The questions were:

WHERE ARE THE CHICKEN BODIES?

WHO OWNS THE FABULOUS RED BURGER BARN?

CHAPTER

AT THREE FORTY-FIVE THE NEXT AFTERNOON, I was in my bedroom closet looking for my detective outfit. Boy, was I glad to get home. Running around in the middle of the night with Jesse had caused a big problem for me in school that day. Namely, I couldn't keep my eyes open. Not even when Ms. Wootechuk reviewed spider parts. I woke up in time to hear her say, "Class dismissed. And don't forget, your completed diagrams are due on Friday."

Friday! Tomorrow! I stared at my spider diagram. Still empty. Except for "HEAD," of course. I picked up my pencil and scrawled a wavy line across its face. "MOUSTACHE," I wrote, in big block letters.

Anybody but Ms. Wootechuk would think that was funny.

I threw on my black shirt and tights and headed down to the parking garage. At four o'clock precisely, I was standing in front of the garbage bins, ready to start searching for the chicken bodies.

Jesse and I had talked it over at lunch-time. We

knew (because of the master key) that the thief must live in the co-op. We also knew that the garbage was picked up on Fridays. This was only Thursday, so chances were good that the bodies were still around. All we had to do was find out whose garbage they were in. Jesse and I would—

Where *was* Jesse anyway? I waited five minutes for him, then ten, pacing in front of the garbage bins. After fifteen minutes, I gave up. Some partner! He was probably still back at school, tying up his dopey shoelaces or something. Who needed him? I'd find the bodies myself.

But first I had to figure out which bin they were most likely to be in. There were a whole bunch of choices. Glass and paper bins—they didn't seem too likely. Neither did the ones for cans. And I couldn't imagine them being in the compost. That left general garbage. Ugh!

General garbage is in a dumpster that's at least as tall as me. It's supposed to be all the stuff that can't be recycled, but some people—the lazy ones—throw everything in. Of all the containers, it's probably the grossest. I shuddered.

"There's only one way, Stevie," I told myself firmly. Taking a deep breath, I began climbing up the side. The dumpster had hooks to grab on to, so it wasn't hard. I clambered over the top and dropped down inside.

Yuck. Double yuck!

I wished I were anywhere else in the entire universe. Some of the bags had split open. Rotten hamburger meat, mucked-up pizza containers, used napkins, mouldy cheese—I was up to my knees in the stuff. Broken toys, too, and worn-out shoes covered in what looked like broken eggs. Scattered in all this mess were piles of fat plastic bags. They could contain anything.

I would have to—ick!—open them up.

For a minute, I considered climbing right back out. Then I thought about my mom. Garbage Busters. My allowance.

Grabbing the nearest plastic bag, I ripped it open. The smell nearly knocked me over. This garbage stunk so bad it must have been there all week, way too long to have the chicken bodies in it. Still, I wasn't going to take any chances. I plunged my hands in and began to root around.

That's when I heard the basement door open. Someone was coming. Hide! But where? There was only—ugh!—one choice. Holding my breath, I burrowed under the nearest pile of plastic bags.

Try to imagine the most horrible and truly disgusting smell that you have ever smelled in your entire life. Then multiply it by about a hundred. You might be getting *close* to what it was like in the middle of that pile. How long, I wondered, could I hold my breath before I passed out?

I heard some footsteps followed by a *whump*, as something dropped into the dumpster. Then, the basement door opened again, and a second set of footsteps came towards the dumpster.

"Howdy, Herb." It was Gertie Wiggins' voice, coming towards the garbage—low and rough, like the other night. "Seems like I always run into you down here."

"Oh, hi, Gertie. I'm just trying to figure out

where to put these old wineglasses. I never use them any more."

I didn't move a muscle. The last thing I needed was to get caught in a dumpster by two of my suspects. But if they kept talking, I was going to suffocate for sure.

"Herb, those glasses are valuable. Worth a fortune, they are. An antique store would give you fifty—maybe a hundred dollars—for them."

"Oh, Gertie, I've got more money than I know what to do with. Here, if you like the glasses, why don't *you* take them?"

"Oh, Herb, I couldn't—"

"Sure you can—"

"No, no, I—"

I put my hand over my nose and took tiny little breaths while they argued.

Finally, Gertie said, "Well, okay, if you really want me to."

They shuffled around the recycling bins for a while, and there was a lot of clanging and tinkling. Finally, I heard the basement door close. I surfaced, gasping for air. I had just managed to get a few breaths of reasonably unstinky air into my lungs when the basement door opened again. I dived back into my pile.

Footsteps again, quick ones this time, and a load of garbage landed right on top of me. As the footsteps disappeared, I struggled out and peeked over the top of the dumpster. Jonathon—hurrying through the door and wearing a lime-green and black exercise suit.

His garbage bag had ripped open, and his

garbage was scattered all over what I was starting to think of as my own personal pile. There were banana peels and carrot ends in it. How come this stuff wasn't in the compost box? And how come Jonathon wasn't recycling these pop tins and jam jars? Just wait till my mom found out. I was grinning at the thought of telling her when I heard the basement door opening again.

This can't be happening, I thought. It's a nightmare. Holding my nose, I wriggled back down into my pile of garbage bags. How many times could I do this and still come out alive?

"Hi, Stevie. Sorry I'm late."

I poked my head out. It was Jesse, peering over the top of the dumpster.

"Eewwww," he said. "Gross, really gross, Stevie. You've got orange peels in your hair and feathers on your nose and—ugh!—what's that stuff on your cheek?"

I wiped my cheek. Something brown and slimy came off on my hand. I didn't know what it was. I didn't want to know.

"Where have you been?" I asked. "We said four o'clock."

"I know. And I said I was sorry. But—I was getting *this* for you." He held up a steaming Cluck Burger. Just the burger. No container. I could smell the fabulous smell even over the stink of the garbage.

"Wow!" I said. "Great, Jesse! How'd you do that?" I lurched to my feet and slipped on the plastic bags.

"It wasn't easy," he said. "I used my powers of

persuasion. Hey, listen, Stevie, your grandfather was looking for you before. Up in the courtyard. Did he find you?"

"My grandfather! My grandfather lives in—wait! What did he look like?"

"Well, you know, like an old man." Jesse shrugged.

"Short? With glasses and big thick eyebrows? Kind of weird-looking?"

"I guess. But what kind of way is that to talk about your grandfather?"

"He's not my grandfather," I said.

Jesse's eyes lit up. "Who is he, Stevie? A suspect?"

"Never mind," I told him, shaking my head. "We'll talk about it later. Right now we've got work to do."

But as I reached for a garbage bag, a shiver ran through me. If Jesse didn't know the old man, then obviously he didn't live in the co-op. Yet he had a key to the apartment building. Who *was* that old guy? And why was he looking for me?

I ripped open the bag. Not too bad. On a one-to-ten scale of grossness, I'd give it about a four. Jesse was still on the outside of the dumpster, looking in.

"Jesse," I said. "The garbage bags are in *here*. If you—"

"Ssshhhhhh," he hissed. "Someone's coming."

I couldn't believe it. Was there some rule, maybe, that everybody in the whole co-op had to take their garbage downstairs at 4:00 p.m. on Thursday afternoon? Jesse disappeared, and I crawled back into my pile. It was beginning to feel like home.

I heard some clinking sounds as stuff got dropped into the glass and metal containers. After a while, there was a soft *whump* in the dumpster. Then, a few minutes later, Jesse's voice.

"He's gone, Stevie. You can come out now."

I crawled slowly out of the garbage. Detecting was beginning to get me down.

"It was Arnie Sykes!" Jesse said eagerly. "He's one of the suspects, isn't he? Quick! Let's check his garbage."

"Okay," I said. "But after that, I'm going home. I've had it!" I was already undoing the twist tie on the bag that Arnie had thrown in. It was one of those jumbo-sized bags, but it was surprisingly light.

What I saw inside made me suck in my breath. "Bingo!" I whispered.

"What? What?" Jesse was jumping up and down and hissing at me from the edge of the dumpster. "I can't see. What's in there?" I dragged the bag over to him and held it open.

He whistled softly. "Stevie!" he said. "It was *him!*"

The bag was filled with the headless bodies of Cluck Burger containers. There must have been fifty of them.

CHAPTER

"THIS IS GREAT!" JESSE YELLED. "THIS IS *fantastic*! Our first day on the job, and we've already got him. What a team!"

I was still staring into the bag, in shock.

"Well, come on," Jesse said. "What are we waiting for? Let's go turn him in. Right now. Let's call the cops."

"Jesse, will you please hold on for just one minute?" I waded over to the edge of the dumpster and began hoisting myself out. "For your information, we haven't caught anybody. What are we going to tell the police? We don't have any proof."

"What do you call that?" He was pointing at the bag of decapitated Cluck Burger containers I'd abandoned in the dumpster.

"Circumstantial evidence," I told him, grateful that I'd read all those mysteries. "It's great that we found it, and it's great that we know who we're after. But it won't do us a bit of good to call the police. Here, give me a hand."

"What's circum—whatever?" asked Jesse, pulling me over the top of the dumpster.

"And—eewww, Stevie—what's that on your hand?" He wiped his hand—the one that had grabbed mine—on the outside of the dumpster. His other hand was still holding the Cluck Burger.

I dropped down beside him and looked at my hands. Pretty slimy. I wiped them on my tights, but it didn't do much good. My tights were almost as filthy as my hands.

"Circumstantial evidence," I told Jesse, "is proof that Arnie *could* have done it. But it's not proof that he *did* do it."

"I don't get it," Jesse said, looking puzzled. "What do we need to prove he really did it?"

"It would help," I said, "to find the money."

I was trying, without much success, to clean myself off. My shoes were covered in some mysterious yellowy-white goo, and my hair was full of plastic foam packing chips. Soggy eggshells clung to my black T-shirt. I had to pick them off one at a time.

"Arnie's probably already deposited the money in the bank," Jesse said gloomily.

"Not if he's smart, he didn't. The police probably told the banks about the robbery. They'll be watching for someone who tries to deposit a lot of small bills. If Arnie's smart, he'll hang on to the money till everything quiets down."

"Yeah," said Jesse, squinting his eyes. "You're right, Stevie. He'll probably hang on to it. So what do we do next? Break into his apartment?"

"Well, we could," I said slowly, remembering my disastrous visit to Gertie's apartment. "But

Arnie spends less time at home than in—"

Jesse's eyes lit up. "His van! Arnie practically lives in his van."

Without another word, we both headed towards the far corner of the parking garage.

"Do you think the money will be there?" Jesse asked.

"Well, it probably won't be lying around on the front seat. But who knows? Arnie doesn't seem to cover his tracks too well."

The van was black—new-looking and gleaming. It had red flames on both sides. In fiery orange letters across the front, it said "Wild Thing."

Jesse tried the driver's door, while I tried the passenger's side. Locked. But when I pulled on the sliding door on the passenger's side, it opened. I poked my head in and looked around.

Weird. In fact, seriously weird.

There were no back seats—just a big open space. All along the walls, somebody—Arnie, I guess—had attached pictures painted on some kind of heavy cloth, like canvas. They weren't like any other pictures I'd ever seen. Strange creatures with long tails, half man and half dog. Birds with long claws and fangs like a tiger. Monster faces on top of frog bodies. I glanced up. The ceiling was a picture, too—crawling with snakes. In the back corners were two of the largest stereo speakers I'd ever seen. They were practically as big as me.

"Wow!" said Jesse from behind me. "This is

really cool." He pushed past me and jumped onto the floor of the van. His feet disappeared.

"Hey, Stevie!" He bounced across the back of the van. "It's a water bed!"

"You're kidding," I said. "In a van?"

"This is great!" he yelled. "Way better than garbage."

The water bed looked like fun, but I didn't see how anybody could have a good time with all those snakes and monsters watching. Besides, we had a job to do and maybe not a whole bunch of time to do it.

"Jesse," I called. "The money. Remember? The robbery?"

"In a minute, Stevie. I just have to try this one more time." He was doing somersaults back and forth across the water bed.

I climbed in, pulled the door shut and bounced over to the front seat. The glove compartment opened right away. Nothing but the usual stuff—papers, a flashlight, a map, a few ballpoint pens. On the floor in front of the passenger seat was a long metal box. I opened it up. Tools. I checked under the passenger seat. Nothing but a few greasy rags. Then I saw the edge of the cardboard box, poking out from under the driver's seat. I pulled it out and opened the flaps.

I froze. Staring back at me was a tangled mass of chicken feet. Real chicken feet. Cut off real chickens. Knobby and yellowish brown with sharp claws at the end. I forced myself to touch one. Yes, they were real all right.

That's when I heard the whistling. It was coming from the far door of the garage. I peeked out the window.

Arnie!

I glanced back. Jesse was stretched out flat, his eyes closed. The water bed rolled in slow waves underneath him.

"Jesse!" I hissed. "Arnie's coming. We've got to get out of here."

His eyes opened wide. I waited for him to jump to his feet, but he just lay there.

"Jesse! Move it!" The whistling was getting louder.

Jesse's arms and legs turned stiff as posts. His eyes looked ready to pop right out of their sockets. Terrific! The perfect time for a panic attack.

"Jesse!" I hissed again. "Come *on*! Right now!"

It was like he was glued to the water bed. Diving into the rear of the van, I hauled him into a sitting position. It wasn't easy. He was as stiff as a block of firewood. I managed to drag him behind the driver's seat and push his legs up against his body. Then I scrunched down beside him. Luckily the driver's seat was huge, with big armrests on the sides.

Then I noticed the water bed. It was heaving up and down in slow waves. Arnie would know right away something was wrong. I put my hand down to try to stop it. I might as well have tried to stop the tide.

The driver's door of the van opened. Jesse made this funny little gulping noise, and I clapped my hand over his mouth.

Maybe Arnie had just come to get something. Maybe the chicken feet. Maybe if we just stayed where we were, as quiet as—Click. And then VRRRRRRRMMMMM! Arnie had started the van.

Suddenly there was a movement right behind Jesse. Something flapping and tugging.

"What the—" Arnie's voice from the front.

The seat belt! Jesse was sitting on it! He stared at me, still frozen stiff. I pulled him off the belt. It flew free, and the buckle must have hit Arnie. I heard him swear. There was a snapping sound as he did himself up.

Jesse's eyes were so big they practically swallowed his face.

The van jerked forward and squealed up the ramp out of the underground lot. We were off!

CHAPTER

A S THE VAN HIT THE SUNLIGHT, I GLANCED around. I couldn't see Arnie, which meant—I hoped—that he couldn't see us. Safe. For now.

Still, sooner or later, Arnie would stop the van. What then?

Our main problem, in the meantime, was the water bed. As soon as the van moved, the surface started rolling and heaving around. I grabbed on to one of the legs of the driver's seat so I wouldn't go flying. Jesse, I was glad to see, was coming alive again. He reached for the other leg of Arnie's seat and held on. His eyes were blinking as if he were waking from a trance. He didn't look frozen any more. Just scared.

A sudden blast of ear-splitting noise shook the van. Jesse and I both jerked upright, letting go of the seat legs to clap our hands over our ears. We rolled towards the back of the van at the same time, banging our heads together as we tried to stop ourselves. I reached out wildly and grabbed for the seat leg. Jesse grabbed for my leg. It was all kind of confused, but somehow we managed to get ourselves back where we started, crouched up against Arnie's seat. This time I ignored the blare of sound and just hung on.

"What's that noise?" Jesse mouthed the words. Or maybe he yelled them. It was impossible to tell.

"Stereo!" I yelled, pointing at the huge speakers at the back.

Jesse's face was screwed up like a prune, and I knew mine must look the same. I figured the noise filling the van was rock music, but I wasn't absolutely sure—it was so loud you couldn't tell. The driver's seat was shaking, and I stuck my head around it, peeking up at Arnie. He was bouncing up and down in his seat to the beat of the music and pounding on the steering wheel as if it were a drum. He was singing, too. At least, I think he was.

I sat back down beside Jesse, and he rolled his eyes at me. The huge black speakers looked like they were ready to explode. I had read that rock stars can get deafened by their own music. Could it happen in a single car ride?

There were no windows in the rear of the van so I couldn't see where we were going. All I knew was that we were travelling along a flat street, which, in my part of Vancouver, means you are not going down to the beach or over a bridge or up to the mountains. We stopped and started a lot and didn't turn, which made me think that we might be on Broadway, the closest busy street to the co-op.

Arnie was a jerky driver, slamming on his brakes and pulling away with a burst of speed. The water bed went crazy each time, and Jesse and I fell against and on top of each other. After one of these jerks, Jesse cupped his hand over my ear and screamed into it.

"I'm not agroudooo rige woog seebooo."

"What?" I screamed back.

"I'm not allowed to rige wigouda seebooo."

"What????"

This time he got his mouth right up against my ear and screamed really slow and clear. "I'm not allowed to ride without a seat belt!"

I stared at him, speechless. What was I supposed to do? Ask Arnie if we could sit up front please, so that Jesse could have a seat belt?

I wished he hadn't mentioned seat belts. It made me think of my mom. What would she say if she could see me? Rattling around in the back of a Wild Thing van, no seat belt on and a lunatic at the wheel. I knew the answer. She'd die. First she'd fall over in a faint, and then she'd die of shock. I tried not to think about it.

Jesse and I held on for a long time. An hour maybe, or more. It was hard to tell—seemed like we'd been rocking and swaying in the back of the van forever. I felt a lump underneath me on the water bed and moved over to see what I was sitting on.

The Cluck Burger. Stone cold. And squished flat. The top crust of the bun was half gone. It had some slimy stuff on it. From my clothes, I guess.

What you have to remember is this: it had

been a long time since I'd eaten lunch. A *long* time. I picked up the Cluck Burger. Carefully, I wiped off the worst of the slime. Jesse made a face. I shrugged and took a huge bite—almost half the burger. Jesse gave me this look like I'd just bitten the head off a live worm.

"Want some?" I yelled, holding the burger in his direction.

He shuddered and shook his head. I took another bite. Not bad, actually, considering what it had been through.

The van was travelling smoothly now. No more stops and starts.

"Where are we?" Jesse screamed in my ear.

"Edge of the city," I yelled back between mouthfuls. "Have to be." I wondered whether it was a good idea to holler out loud that way. If Arnie ever turned off his stereo, Jesse and I would be left screeching at each other in the silence.

"We're leaving Vancouver?" Jesse looked like he was on his way back to his frozen state, so I quickly yelled, "No, no. Just the outskirts."

He didn't look convinced. He huddled down, eyes enormous, shoulders stiff, hands clenched.

I decided to ignore Jesse and try to check out the back of the van—the way Samantha Sams does in *The Runaway Truck Mystery*. She solves the whole mystery in one short ride and jumps to safety just seconds before the truck hurtles over a cliff. I didn't want my ride in Arnie's van to be *that* exciting. Still, might as well use this time to do a bit of detecting.

All along each side, things were stuffed into the cracks between the water bed and the van wall. Most of the stuff looked like rubbish, but it was worth checking out. Swallowing the last few mouthfuls of Cluck Burger, I got on my hands and knees. I kept an eye on the back of Arnie's seat, ready to drop to my stomach if I saw any movement. Could he see me in the rear-view mirror? I hoped not. The water bed rolled and heaved. It was like crawling across a trampoline while somebody else jumps on it.

This is what I found on the first side I tried:

- A squashed tissue box, empty
- Seven chocolate-bar wrappers, crumpled
- Four empty pop cans
- Half a red licorice, slightly dirt-smeared
- An old long-sleeved shirt, white and covered in paint smears
- A paperback book, ragged-looking, called *Horror on Maple Avenue*

Not much to learn except that Arnie was a slob and ate junk food. I took a chew of the licorice and offered the rest to Jesse. He made another face at me. What a picky eater!

Scarfing down the rest of the licorice, I crawled to the other side of the water bed, tumbling over a couple of times on the way. The first thing I found was a plastic bag. It was full, but light. More cut-up Cluck Burger packages? I opened it and looked inside.

Feathers! A whole bagful. Chicken feathers, maybe? From the dead chickens whose feet were in the cardboard box under Arnie's seat?

Then I looked more closely. The feathers were all sizes and colours. Some were five or six inches long; others were soft and tiny. There were black feathers and white feathers and reddish feathers and yellow feathers.

What was Arnie Sykes doing with a bagful of feathers? He didn't look like the kind of guy who stuffed pillows for a hobby.

I put the bag of feathers aside and saw a long leather-like case underneath. Golf clubs? A pool cue? I realized that I didn't know very much about Arnie. I pulled open the zipper. As soon as I saw the metal, I knew what it was. Closing the zipper, I crawled back to Jesse as fast as I could.

"Arnie's got a gun!" I screamed.

Big mistake. Jesse's legs shot out straight in front of him and his knees locked into place. His arms stiffened into ramrods at his sides. His eyes stared straight ahead.

Oh no. Jesse! Don't do this. Not again.

I was starting to get worried. We were bumping along on some kind of country road, miles from home and getting farther every minute. Jesse was in terrible shape, and Arnie obviously wasn't going to drive forever. Behind us was this rifle, or whatever it was. What would happen when we stopped?

Just then the van turned a corner, rocked its way over a couple of big bumps and skidded to a halt. After a few seconds, the stereo noise ended with a suddenness that made my ears ring. I covered Jesse's mouth with my hand and waited.

CHAPTER

I T WAS PROBABLY ONLY A FEW SECONDS BEFORE Arnie opened his door, but it felt like an hour.

"Yo! Slug!" he said as he stepped out of the van. "How you doing, man? You been waiting long?"

"Nah," said a rough nasal voice, grown-up and male. "Just ten minutes or so. Looks good, Arnie. I already saw some geese. There's grouse around here, too. I feel lucky."

Grouse. Geese. That's what the gun was for. They were here to go hunting. I peeked cautiously over the driver's seat. Through the front window of the van, I could see a marshy-looking flatland with low thick bushes all around and thin trees in the distance. Not a building anywhere. Or a person. Except for Arnie, that is. And his friend, Slug.

They were standing in front of the van with their backs to me. Slug's head was completely shaved, but the rest of him was as hairy as a gorilla. He was even bigger than Arnie, if that were possible, with monstrous shoulders and arms like tree trunks. Hairy tree trunks. His T-shirt and pants were black, and he was wearing a big hoop earring in one ear.

A shiver ran down my spine and kept going, all the way to my toes. Arnie and Slug were not about to wander off quietly into the bush, allowing me and Jesse to sneak away. Arnie wasn't going *anywhere* without his gun. And there it was, stashed right next to my big toe.

Arnie and Slug were also not going to be pleased to find a couple of kids stowed away on their hunting expedition. I figured they'd be mad. Just how mad, I wasn't sure. What if Arnie guessed *why* we had snuck into his van?

"It's the strangest thing." Arnie sounded puzzled. "I cleaned my van up just last week and got rid of a lot of crap. Today I get in, and you know what? It stinks like a garbage truck."

Slug laughed. Not a pleasant sound.

I looked down at my detective outfit. The goo and slime had dried now, and a light crust covered most of my T-shirt and tights. I grabbed the top of my T-shirt and sniffed it. Ugghhh! Garbage truck.

"Well, whaddaya say, Arnie?" Slug sounded eager now. "You ready to bag a few birds?"

My whole body tensed. I turned to Jesse. He was staring straight ahead, as rigid as if he were carved out of stone.

"Jesse," I hissed. "We only get one chance here. When those guys open the door, we have to run. Now move it!"

I headed for the back of the van and got into

a crouch. There was no way to know which door Arnie would open, but I was hoping for one of the doors at the front of the van. I stared at the handles of the back doors, ready to grab one and twist it. There was a shuffling noise behind me. Jesse. He joined me in a runner's crouch.

Suddenly the back doors flew open. Arnie and Slug stood there right in front of us, looking mean as snakes and ugly as toads. When they saw me and Jesse, their jaws dropped open. For a second, nobody moved. Then I followed my first instinct. Screaming and flailing my arms, I leaped straight at them.

"Gyaaaahhhhh!" I screeched, hurling my body between them. They reeled back in shock, leaving a space for me — and Jesse, who was right behind me and screeching, too — to charge through, making a beeline for the bushes.

"Gyaaaaaahhhhhhh!" we both screamed as we threw ourselves into the closest clump of green.

Blackberry bushes! Dozens of thorns tore into my arms as I thrashed through. I could hear Slug and Arnie behind me, yelling "Hey!" I kept running. When it came to a choice between blackberry bushes or Slug and Arnie, I'd take the bushes any day.

"Gyaaaahhhhh!" I yelled again, this time because of the thorns tearing into my skin. I scrambled over a low-lying bush and fell to one knee. Jumping up, I ran and fell again. The blackberry brambles seemed to go on forever

112

with little patches of clear space in between. I could hear Jesse behind me, yelling "Ow! Ow! Ow! Ow!"

From way behind us, back in the bushes, I heard another voice — Arnie's or Slug's, I couldn't tell which. "Hey! Hey, you little brats! Come back here!" But the sound was distant. Arnie and Slug didn't seem to be following. I wasn't surprised. If I weren't being chased by two huge bozos with guns, I wouldn't run through those bushes either.

I pushed through a tangle of brambles and came to a clear spot. Panting heavily, I stopped. Jesse dragged himself out of a bush and fell to his knees in front of me.

"Know what, Stevie?" he gasped. "I'm not ... absolutely sure ... I *want* ... to be a detective." His hat was twisted halfway around, and his arms and face were covered with blackberry juice and scratches.

I sat down beside him. "Detective work isn't supposed to be like this," I told him. "It's never like this in books."

Jesse collapsed onto his stomach and then immediately leaped up again. "Yow!" he yelled. A baby blackberry bush was clinging to the front of his T-shirt. He began to pick it off, carefully, with two fingers.

"Shhh — " I said. "Listen!"

We both stopped breathing. Behind us, we could hear crashing and stomping. Also some swear words that are too rude to repeat here.

"Oh my gosh," said Jesse. "They're coming!"

"Let's go!" I grabbed his arm and hauled him to his feet before he could freeze up again.

We started creeping through the bushes, away from the van, trying to work our way around the blackberry thorns instead of ploughing right through them. Jesse grumbled the whole way and kept saying "Ow" and "Yowch" every time a thorn got him, until I pointed out that Arnie and Slug were probably following his voice. That shut him up. We crept on slowly, stopping now and then to listen for Slug and Arnie. Their voices were getting dimmer. After a while, they disappeared.

But now I had a new worry. Jesse and I were moving farther and farther away from the road. We had made our way out of the blackberry bushes and into a patch of alder trees. It was getting late, and soon it would be dark. The idea of spending the night out in the woods wasn't very appealing.

"Hey, Stevie," said Jesse, as if he were reading my mind, "are we lost?" He sounded nervous.

"No way," I told him, crossing my fingers behind my back. "I know exactly where we're going. Straight ahead, through these trees." One thing I had discovered about Jesse Kulniki— he's not exactly reliable in a crisis. I figured I'd better keep any bad news to myself.

Just as well, too, because about fifteen minutes later, we came out the other side of the trees. Right in front of us was another road. Not very big, it's true—just a little gravel lane, really. But at least we were out of the woods.

"Terrific, Stevie," said Jesse, looking impressed. "Which way now?"

"Uh ... left," I said. Why not? Either way, the road wound off into thick clumps of trees with no signs of a house. Jesse and I started hiking down the road to the left.

Now that we were out in the open, the wind was stronger and the air had turned cooler—a lot cooler. I shivered as a few raindrops hit me. The sky was grey-black, full of thick, heavy clouds that looked ready to dump a huge storm right on top of us.

Jesse, I thought. It was *his* fault. If he hadn't frozen up that way in the underground parking lot, we would never have—

"Stevie?"

"Uh-huh?"

"I'm sorry. I mean, I know it's my fault that we're stuck out here."

"That's okay," I said. I was kind of surprised to hear myself say that. But it's hard to stay mad at someone who's apologizing to you.

"Stevie?"

"Uh-huh?"

"Are you cold?"

"Freezing."

"Me, too. Wish I had a jacket."

I glanced over at him. His shoulders were shaking under his T-shirt, and his arms—folded across his chest—were covered in goose bumps. The raindrops were coming down harder now, and the road was slick and wet. It really was going to be a storm.

"Jesse?"

"Uh-huh?"

"What kind of jacket?"

"A big, long one," he said, "with thick furry lining." He was slapping his arms to warm them up.

"Yeah," I said, clenching my teeth so they wouldn't rattle. "And a hood. A fat, warm, waterproof hood."

"And gloves," Jesse said, rubbing his hands. "Big, thick gloves."

We looked at each other and grinned. Both of us were totally drenched. Our T-shirts were plastered against our skin. Jesse's baseball cap looked droopy, and my wet hair straggled down my face.

"Here!" Jesse said, taking off his baseball cap and plopping it onto my head. I started to say no, but he shook his head. "Keep it," he said. "You deserve it."

The rain was really coming down now, hitting the gravel in big plops and bouncing up again. We passed two houses, both dark, with no cars in the driveways. We could only see the road for a short way in front of us. Soon, the sun would go down entirely, leaving us in pitch black.

"Hey, Stevie?" Jesse was kicking a stone down the road. In spite of our miserable condition, he sounded kind of perky.

"Uh-huh?"

"We did pretty great back there, didn't we?

Scaring those guys that way when we jumped out of the van."

Slug and Arnie couldn't have looked more shocked if a couple of chimpanzees had leaped out at them. I laughed. "Yeah," I said. "We were pretty good, all right."

"Watch this!"

He ran ahead of me down the road and disappeared behind a bush. What now? Suddenly, he leaped out, charging straight at me. He had this fierce, crazy expression on his face—like a wolf that's just been let out of a cage—and both hands were flailing around above his head.

"Gyaaaaahhhhh!" he screamed, running around me in circles. "Gyaaaahhhh, Slug! Gyaaaaaahhhhhh, Arnie!"

His teeth were bared like fangs, and his eyes were bugging out. No wonder Arnie and Slug had been stunned! When Jesse saw me laughing, he got really carried away.

"Take that, you creep!" he yelled, aiming a swift kick at a tall weed by the side of the road. "Lemme go, you big jerk!" he screamed up into the rain.

I'm not exactly sure how it happened, but soon we were *both* dancing around on the gravel road, yelling "Gyaaahhh" and "Take that!" I laughed so hard I tripped over a rock and fell on my backside into this huge pothole full of water—which struck Jesse, I guess, as the funniest thing he'd ever seen, because that's when *he* fell down.

So there we were, both of us rolling in the mud and screaming with laughter, while all around, the wind howled and wailed. Even the sky got into the act. It opened up with a loud crack of thunder and dumped what must have been a whole cloudful of rain right on top of Jesse and me.

Didn't matter. We couldn't get any wetter. Or dirtier.

"Come on," I said finally, picking myself up and brushing off my tights. They were so disgusting—filthy, ragged, soaking wet—that I laughed again.

"Hey, Stevie," said Jesse. "Have you noticed something? It's almost dark out."

I looked around and stopped laughing. Jesse was right. Within minutes, we wouldn't be able to see more than a few feet ahead of us.

"Hey, look!" I said. "There's an intersection up there, and a stop sign. Maybe there are some street signs or directions or something."

All I could think of as we hurried down that dark, rainy road was how glad I was not to be doing this alone. Of course, if I had been alone, I never would have gotten trapped in Arnie's van in the first place. On the other hand, if I hadn't gotten trapped in the van, I never would have found the box of chicken feet and the bag of feathers.

"Hey, Jesse!" I said, remembering that he didn't even know. "You'll never guess what I found in Arnie's van."

"What? More clues?"

I told him about the feathers and the feet.

"Ewww," he said. "That's gross. What a horrible thing to do to a chicken."

"Never mind the chicken," I said. "Anyway, it must have been a whole bunch of chickens. And other birds, too. The thing I want to know is—why? What does Arnie do with this stuff?"

"Something nasty, that's for sure. You know, like the garbage through your door? Maybe he was planning to tie the chicken feet to your bicycle spokes."

"Now that would be *really* dumb," I said, trying to picture it. "Why would he want to do that?"

"Because he's nuts, that's why. Only someone who's nuts would go around shooting perfectly innocent birds. Birds that never did anybody a bit of harm, birds that—"

"It just doesn't add up," I interrupted quickly. "Somehow this whole thing is connected to the Red Barn. I'm *sure* of it. Does Arnie have any connection with the Red Barn?"

"He eats there," said Jesse. "But then, so do tons of other people. Even Gertie eats there sometimes. I've seen—"

"Ssshhhh—" I said. The faint sound of a car motor came from behind us. It was heading this way. Arnie and Slug?

We were almost at the intersection. "Quick!" I said, grabbing Jesse's hand and jumping into the ditch beside the stop sign. It was full of tall grass and bullrushes. We crouched down and waited as two bright lights glowed closer and closer through the rain.

A rattle-bang old farm truck came slowly into view, creeping along the road like a lame dog. It creaked and chugged like it was ready for the scrap heap. As it pulled up at the stop sign, I whispered "Now!" and grabbed Jesse's arm. Keeping low, we raced out of the ditch and pulled ourselves onto the back of the truck, landing on some rough sacks full of something lumpy and knobby.

"Potatoes," said Jesse, pointing at the printing on the bags.

The truck pulled away with a clang and a rumble, and the rain began to hit us in wind-driven sheets. Soon I was numb with cold. I tried to ask Jesse if he had any ideas, but my teeth were chattering so hard I couldn't get the words out. To make things worse, I was discovering that no matter how you squirm, you just can't get comfy on a sack of potatoes. Jesse and I didn't talk. We just hung on. The truck finally came out on a highway and travelled along it for a long time before pulling off onto some smaller streets.

"Look!" said Jesse. He was pointing at an elevated railway almost directly overhead.

"The Sky Train!" I said. "Watch for a station."

The Sky Train in Vancouver is like the subway in other cities. The difference is that it travels way up above the ground. If we could find a station, we could get home.

"There!" I said. As the truck slowly rounded a corner, we leaped off. I stumbled as I landed and fell to one knee. Another tear in my tights and a new scrape. Nothing major.

"We'll be home in less than an hour," I told Jesse. He chattered his teeth at me in reply.

We limped stiffly up to the automatic ticket machines.

"Stick some money in, Stevie," said Jesse, "and hurry. I'm practically a Popsicle."

A horrible thought hit me. "I don't *have* any money," I said. "Don't you?"

"Nothing!" said Jesse. Goose bumps stood up on his arms like raisins. "Not a cent."

I thought about it. The way the Sky Train works is you buy a ticket from the machine and get on the train. Sometimes somebody comes around to check your ticket, but not very often. "Let's just get on," I said. "Probably nobody will check anyway."

Jesse looked horrified. "We can't do that," he said. "That's stealing. If we do that, we're as bad as Arnie. We can't—"

"Jesse!" I wailed. "Are you trying to drive me crazy? Let's just get on the train, okay? Tomorrow we'll write a nice letter to the transit company and send them the money for our fares."

He crossed his arms and stuck out his lower lip. "No!" he said. "I won't do it."

I sighed and sat down on a bench. "Okay. Fine. How do you suggest we get home?"

His brow wrinkled in thought. Suddenly his eyes lit up. "We'll busk," he said.

"What?"

"We'll stand here and sing. I'll put my hat down, and people will throw money in it."

"Uh-uh," I said, shaking my 'head. "Not me. No way."

"Oh, Stevie," he said. "There's nothing to it."

He grabbed the baseball cap off my head, plunked it down on the pavement and started to sing. The few people walking by stared at him curiously.

Since you went and left me—

I don't know what to do—

I sat up, surprised. Jesse's voice was good. *Very* good. If he had a guitar, he might even be terrific.

I feel like I'm falling to pieces—

Two ladies in fancy coats and hats came walking down the platform. They looked older than my mom but younger than my grandma. They stopped and stared at Jesse.

'Cause all I need is you.

"Sings like an angel, doesn't he, Franny?" said one of the ladies.

"He surely does, Maudie," said the other in a cheerful voice. "Just like Elvis."

I really need you, baby—

They smiled and dropped some coins in Jesse's hat. As soon as they left, we dived at the hat.

"Great!" said Jesse. "Eighty cents."

"Not enough," I said. "Sing some more."

I sat back down on my bench, slapping at my arms to warm them, while Jesse launched into another song.

❖ ❖ ❖

Half an hour later, we were riding the Sky Train, enjoying the warmth of the heater as it crept through our wet clothes. Each of us had $3.23. Jesse had been hard to stop once he got started, and he had insisted on dividing the money up evenly.

"Wish people would give us bills instead of coins," Jesse said. His pocket was bulging and drooping from the weight of the coins.

"I know what you mean," I said. My money was in my wrist-wallet, and it felt like my whole arm was dragging on the ground. I took the coins out and jingled them around. The clinking and the weight reminded me of something. What? I jingled them again.

"What are you doing?" Jesse asked.

"Thinking," I said. "About how heavy a bunch of coins is—even just $3.23 in change. I was remembering how the thief left all those rolls of coins on our kitchen table."

"So?"

"So maybe that's *why* the thief left the coins behind. Because they're so heavy. Maybe he didn't want to carry them. Or *couldn't* carry them."

"Stevie, why do you keep saying 'the thief'? We know it's Arnie."

"I'm not so sure. Arnie's a big guy. He could carry a huge sack of coins if he wanted to. It just doesn't make sense."

Jesse shrugged. "Maybe we just can't expect every single thing to make sense."

"But it has to," I said. "A mystery is like a jigsaw puzzle. It all has to fit together. And some of these pieces just don't fit."

"Maybe Arnie's not working by himself," said Jesse. "You *did* see him talking to Gertie the other day, right? Gertie's little and old. I bet she couldn't carry a big sack of coins."

"Right," I said. "And then there's Old Eyebrows, too—that strange old guy who's been spying on me. I still haven't figured out who he is."

"Maybe they're a gang!" said Jesse. "Maybe they're all in it together."

We both sat silently for a few minutes. I tried to get the pieces to fit, but something was wrong. Or missing.

"Oh boy," Jesse said.

"What?"

"My mother. I told her I was just going out for a few minutes. Oh boy. She's going to flip right out."

Uh, oh. If Jesse's mother was going to flip out, *mine* would be off the planet. I was sure glad we were in this together. If I was going to get into trouble, at least I wouldn't get into it alone.

"Your mom's a worry-wart, too, huh?" I said.

"Yup." Jesse looked glum.

"How about your dad? Does he flip out over stuff like this?" I'd never seen Jesse's dad. I figured he and Jesse's mom must be divorced.

"There's just me and my mom. My dad died before I was two."

"Oh," I said, not knowing what else to say. "Do you miss him?"

"Not really. I mean, I didn't really know him or anything. It's always been just me and my mom. Do you have a dad?"

I explained about my dad and the mountain goats in the Yukon. It was hard not to sound grouchy about it.

"Gee," he said, when I'd finished. "You're really lucky, Stevie."

"Lucky!" I snorted. "Lucky how?"

"Don't you go with him sometimes? Where there's bears and mountains and eagles and beavers and moose and everything? I wish—" He stopped and stared out the window.

I felt really funny. Jesse was right. I *could* do all that. My dad took me hiking and fishing every chance he got. My life wasn't exactly the way I wanted it, but I guess there *were* a few good things.

As we left the Sky Train station, there was something I had to say to Jesse. But I felt a bit shy about it.

"Jesse," I said. "You were a real pain in the butt when we were in the van." No, no, no. That's not what I wanted to say.

"I know," he said, hanging his head. "I already *said* I was sorry, didn't I?"

"Actually, that's not what I meant. What I meant is—I'm glad you're my partner. I had the most fun today that I've had in a long time." It was true. I hadn't had so much fun since before I'd changed schools.

"Really?" he said, lifting his head and grinning at me. "You think I'm fun?"

"The funnest," I said.

"You, too, Stevie," he said, giving me a little punch on the arm. "You're the funnest, too."

I smiled. But as we jumped onto the bus that would take us the final lap of the way home, I remembered my mom. And Jesse's mom. Would *they* think the evening had been fun?

And what about Arnie? I bet *he* wasn't in a fun mood. He was probably home by now. Him, and maybe Slug, too. Hanging around the co-op. Waiting.

CHAPTER

T HE MOMENT WE STEPPED INTO THE COURT-
yard, I knew I was in serious trouble.
Every single light in our town house was
on, even in the bedrooms — pretty strange
because my mom has a thing about not wasting
electricity. The front door was wide open, too; it
was swinging back and forth in the wind and
rain. I could see what looked like crowds of
people inside.

"Uh, oh," I said, my heart sinking.

"Maybe it's not what you think," said Jesse in
a hopeful voice. "Maybe she's throwing a party.
Maybe she hasn't even noticed that you're
gone."

Jesse and I walked through the open door. I
was amazed. It *did* look like a party. There
were people everywhere — on the couch, in
chairs, standing in the kitchen doorway — all
jabbering at once. One by one, their expressions
changed as they caught sight of Jesse and me.
The living room became as silent as a cemetery.

Then a whole bunch of people rushed us, all
talking at once so we couldn't understand a

word. Some of them were yelling, and one woman looked like she was ready to cry.

"Stephanie!" shrieked my mom. Pushing her way through the crowd, she threw her arms around me. "Where have you *been*?" she squeaked in my ear. Her voice was so high-pitched it almost disappeared.

Right behind her was Mrs. Kulniki, looking thin and white. She grabbed Jesse and clutched him to her tightly, without saying a word.

I looked over my mom's shoulder at the rest of the crowd. A whole bunch of Garbage Busters were there, staring at Jesse and me as if we had just returned from the grave. There were people from the co-op, too — Maisie Sebastian, a lawyer who lives next door, and Irene and David Wong from across the court-yard. And Jonathon, of course, looking his handsomest in a purple and blue aerobics suit.

Across the room — sitting in the stuffed green chair and mumbling away to herself — was Gertie Wiggins. I sucked in my breath. What was *she* doing here? Her eyes narrowed when she caught sight of me. Then she looked away, still mumbling.

Off in the other corner were a couple of blue uniforms. Police! A tall, balding policeman and a sandy-haired policewoman with freckles and round glasses were watching Jesse and me in silence.

"Where have you *been*?" my mom repeated. "It's after eleven. You disappeared at four o'clock without a word to anyone."

I thought fast. "On the Sky Train," I said, smiling a no-big-deal kind of smile. No one smiled back.

"On the *Sky Train*? You just went for a seven-hour ride on the Sky Train? Without saying anything? Without phoning?" My mom was moving out of the I'm-so-grateful-you're-alive stage. Soon she'd get to the you-could-have-been-killed stage. I wondered how long it would take her to reach the I'm-so-mad-I-could-kill-you stage. She was holding me tightly by both shoulders now, as if she were afraid to let go. Her hair was wild, and she had a big smear of dirt and tears down one cheek, like she'd been crying.

Jonathon came up behind her and put an arm around her shoulder. "There, there, Valerie," he said. "All's well that ends well. Young lady, your mother has been very worried about you."

"I can *see* that!" I snapped. I couldn't help it. I hate being called *young lady*.

"Stevie!" my mom said.

"Sorry, Mom."

"Excuse me," said the policewoman, interrupting. She smiled at Jesse and me as if it wasn't the worst crime in the world to stay out till eleven without telling your mother. Maybe she recognized us as fellow detectives. "I'm glad you two are back safely. If there's nothing else, my partner and I had better be getting along now."

"Wait!" said Jesse, grabbing at her arm. "There *is* something else."

I stared at him so hard I'm surprised I didn't bore two holes in his face. I tried thought-transfer. Don't tell, I thought. Don't tell about Arnie.

"What is it?" said the policewoman, turning to Jesse with a pleasant smile.

"Oh...uh, nothing," said Jesse, looking at me and scratching his head. "That is...I, uh, forget."

"Well, if you remember, give us a call," said the policeman. He nodded goodbye, and the two of them left.

"Now, Jesse," said Mrs. Kulniki in a stern voice. "You've got a lot of explaining to do."

"There's nothing to explain," said Jesse, glancing at me out of the corner of his eye. "Like Stevie said, we went riding on the Sky Train, and we just forgot the time."

"Forgot the time?" said Mom. "*Forgot the time*? For seven hours?" You would have thought we'd disappeared for seven years. She was turning me around now and looking me over. "Stevie, what on *earth* happened to you? Look at your clothes. They're filthy. And ripped, too. Look at this! Holes all over the place. And—oh, Stevie—you've been hurt." Now she was down on the floor, inspecting the damage to my right knee.

"Mom," I said. "It's nothing. Really. I'm fine. I fell down, that's all."

"Fell down?" said my mom. "You look like you fell into a garbage compactor."

Jesse and I looked at each other. I bit the inside of my lip, hard. This was *not* a good time to laugh.

Gertie Wiggins shuffled into the middle of the room. "Well, I don't know about the rest of you," she said in an annoyed voice, "but I've got better things to do than sit around here jawing all night." Pushing past Jonathon, she disappeared out the door.

The rest of the co-op people and the Garbage Busters started to leave then, too. My mom went to the door to thank them and say how sorry she was to have troubled them. Jonathon stood beside her, shaking people's hands and thanking them.

Finally, only Jesse and his mother and Jonathon were left. Mrs. Kulniki turned as she reached the door, and she and my mom collapsed together into a big hug.

"Oh, Valerie," said Mrs. Kulniki with a catch in her voice. "I don't know what I would have done without you."

"No, no, Marcia," my mom said, patting her on the back. "You were a pillar of strength. I don't know how to thank you." They walked through the door, arm in arm.

Jesse and I stared at each other, our mouths hanging open. Just yesterday, our moms had been strangers, hissing at each other in front of the Red Barn. Now they looked like they'd been buddies since kindergarten.

"Jesse?" called Mrs. Kulniki, poking her head back in the door. "What are you waiting for? Stephanie and her mother need to get some sleep."

Jesse shrugged at me, and they were gone,

leaving me and my mom alone. Except for Jonathon, of course.

My mom gave me her now-we're-going-to-have-a-serious-talk look.

"You've got some explaining to do, young lady." Reaching into her pocket, she pulled out a white label. It said "HELLO, MY NAME IS" and then, in my handwriting, "STEVIE DIAMOND, DETECTIVE."

"That's my personal private property," I sputtered. "That's—"

"I told you, Stevie, this isn't a game. Whatever you've been doing with this detective business could be very dangerous. There's someone out there who's desperate to stop the Garbage Busters' campaign. Someone who—" She closed her eyes and shook her head, too upset to go on.

"I think we'd better show her, Valerie," said Jonathon, patting her shoulder.

"Show me what?"

"You're right," said my mom, pulling herself together. The next thing I knew, the three of us were crossing the courtyard. Jonathon's apartment was the very last one on the second floor. His door is around a corner at the end, so it wasn't until we turned the corner that I saw it. In big red letters on his door, someone had smeared:

STOP THE DEMONSTRATIONS!

"Do you understand what was *used* to write that message?" asked Jonathon in a quiet voice.

"Oh, Jonathon, no," said my mom. "The

132

message itself is bad enough. We don't want to scare Stevie."

That's when I realized that my mom and Jonathon both thought the same thing — that the message was written in blood! But then, that's because they were over thirty. People over thirty — especially if they eat health food — almost never use the stuff smeared on Jonathon's door.

I stuck out my finger, picked up some of an "S" and tasted it.

"Aaaggghh!" my mother screamed. "Stevie!"

"Relax, Mom," I said. "It's just ketchup."

"Ketchup?" She looked confused.

"Yeah," I said. "That gooey red stuff people put on hamburgers and French fries and eggs and—"

"I *know* what ketchup is." She stuck out her finger and tasted an "E." Then she laughed. "Jonathon, Stevie's right. It *is* ketchup."

"Oh," said Jonathon. "Ketchup, is it?" He laughed, too, but I could tell he didn't get the joke.

"When did you discover this stuff on your door, Jonathon?" Maybe if I knew when it happened, I could figure out who did it.

"About an hour ago," he said. "I came home to—"

"Stevie!" my mom interrupted. "Is this more of your amateur detective stuff? When are you going to see that this is dangerous? You could get hurt."

I thought about my stubbed toe. And the

scratches on my arms. And my scraped knee. If only she knew.

"Tell her about the call." Jonathon's voice was quiet.

My mom took a deep breath. "Jonathon received one of those crank phone calls this afternoon."

"Really?" I said. "The weird ones? Was there a voice? Did you hear anything?"

Jonathon glanced at my mom and then nodded. "I'm afraid so."

"Jonathon, you didn't tell me!" My mom was biting her nails, something she never does. "What kind of voice?"

"I didn't want to scare you, Valerie. He sounded kind of rough. He said if we kept looking for trouble, we'd get it."

"He?" I said quickly. "You're sure it was a he?"

"Stee-vee! Will you cut it *out*?" Mom glared at me.

Jonathon took both her hands in his. "Valerie, I'm not worried about myself. But I *am* worried about you. And you have a child to think of. You shouldn't be taking risks like this." He did look worried.

My mom tried to smile. "Maybe you're right, Jonathon," she said. "Things are getting out of hand. I'll sleep on it."

She thanked Jonathon again and we left. As we crossed the courtyard to our town house, I asked her about something that had been bothering me ever since I'd come home.

"What was Gertie Wiggins doing at our place

tonight?" I couldn't imagine my mom asking Gertie to help hunt for me and Jesse.

"Well, when I discovered that label of yours, I figured you must be poking around, playing detective. I remembered how suspicious you were of Gertie the other day, so I went over to check. Gertie hadn't seen you, of course. But then she followed me back to our house. She was wandering in and out all evening."

"She hangs around a lot," I said. "Every time I—"

"Oh my gosh!" said my mom, clapping her hand over her mouth. "Your father!"

"Dad? What about him?"

"I was in such a panic about you being gone that I phoned him in Whitehorse. About an hour ago. Oh, Stevie, you have to call him right away and tell him you're okay."

❖ ❖ ❖

My dad's pretty relaxed most of the time, but even he sounded tense as I talked to him on the phone. "You can't just wander off like that, Steph. We were very worried about you."

"I know, Dad," I said. "And I'm really sorry. But—but—you've got something a whole lot worse to worry about." There was my mouth, taking off on its own again.

"What is it, Steph? What do I have to worry about?"

Now that I'd said that much, I couldn't stop. "It's Jonathon," I said bluntly.

"Jonathon?" I could tell Dad had never heard of him.

"Yeah," I said. "He's a Garbage Buster, and he lives here in the co-op, and he wears exercise outfits, and he had ketchup smeared all over his door tonight and—"

"Whoa!" said my dad, laughing. "Just a minute. What's all this got to do with me?"

"He's hanging around Mom all the time," I said. "You better get back here right away or...or..."

"Or what?"

"Or they might get married."

"Married?" I could hear the amazement in my dad's voice, all the way from Whitehorse. "Your mom's already married. To me. Remember?"

"Oh, sure," I said. "She's married to you *now*. But what about next month? Or next year?"

"Hmmm," said my dad. "Sounds serious. Tell you what, Steph. I've almost finished up here. I could probably get away in a couple of weeks."

"*Two weeks*! They'll probably be engaged by then. You don't know what a slick guy this Jonathon is, Dad. He's a real super smoothie. Mom's delirious about him."

"Delirious, eh? I'll do my best, Steph."

"Stevie, Dad. Everybody calls me Stevie now."

"Okay, Stevie. See you soon as I can."

As soon as I got off the phone, I felt horrible pangs in my stomach. Pangs of sadness, maybe? From missing my dad? Pangs of guilt from exaggerating about Jonathon?

Nope. Much simpler—pangs of *hunger*. The

cold and half-mashed Cluck Burger I'd eaten in Arnie's van was just a dim memory now. There was only one thing to do.

"Stevie?" came my mom's voice from her bedroom. "What are you up to out there?"

"Just getting a snack, Mom," I called from the kitchen, where I was busy constructing one of my famous toasted triple-decker sandwiches. The bottom layer was tomatoes, cream cheese and alfalfa sprouts; the middle layer was cheddar cheese and olives; and the top layer was mayo and fat chunks of avocado. The slices of rye bread were toasted golden brown and slathered with melting butter.

Jesse would be proud of me, I thought. No meat. Of course, if there'd been any salami or ham in the fridge, my sandwich would have been stuffed fat with it.

"Stevie?" my mom called again. "Finish eating and get right to sleep, you hear? No more detecting tonight."

"Sure thing, Mom." For once, I could be perfectly truthful. After all, it was after midnight. Arnie must be home and asleep. And Gertie and Herb and all the other suspects would have gone to bed, too. As soon as I'd finished my sandwich, I'd get out of my disgusting clothes and under some warm cozy quilts.

I smiled as I took my first bite. It was *impossible* for anything else to happen that night. At least, that's what I figured.

I figured wrong.

CHAPTER

I GUESS I'LL NEVER KNOW WHAT WOKE ME OUT OF a sound sleep just two hours later. Maybe it was the rain, pounding against my bedroom window. Maybe it was some special sense that only detectives have. Or maybe waking up at three a.m. was getting to be a habit.

Whatever it was, I couldn't fall asleep again, no matter how hard I tried. After a few minutes, I gave up and turned on my bed light. The sudden brightness made me blink, and I looked down at my watch. It was covered by my wrist-wallet, which I'd been too tired to take off.

Click!

That's just how it happened. Something clicked in my mind, like the insides of a combination lock when you get the right combination. Click, and then click again. I had it! The missing piece to the puzzle.

I knew now—almost for sure—who the thief was. But who would believe me?

I sat up in bed, my mind racing. Through the window came a gentle *ruh*-ruh-*ruh*-ruh-*rooooo*. I glanced out. There it was—the rooster sign with its egg just starting to crack open.

Wait a minute! I stopped and looked out the window again. Yes! The light *was* on. I pushed aside the wrist-wallet and looked at my watch: 3:05 a.m. The Red Barn closed every night at 10:00 p.m., and the staff left about an hour later. The light was always out by midnight. How come it was on now?

I flashed back to something Jesse had said, just twenty-four hours earlier. Closing my eyes, I tried to remember his exact words: "All I know is, my mom was told to leave the receipts out one night because the owner was coming by to check them. Late. After the restaurant closed."

Then I remembered something else. That sound I'd heard over the phone the time I answered it in the middle of the night—I knew it was something familiar, something I heard all the time. Now I knew what it was. The Red Barn rooster—crowing over the phone. The crank caller had been phoning from *inside the Red Barn*!

I looked out the window at the light in the restaurant window. This was it—my big chance. I had no proof, but as sure as my name was Stevie Diamond, I knew one thing: the thief and the owner of the Red Barn were the same person. And I knew who that person was. But how could I prove it?

There was only one thing to do.

I jumped out of bed and pulled on a pair of dark blue jeans and a green sweater. A chill ran through me that had nothing to do with being cold. As I headed for the front door, I promised myself to be extra careful. I'd get Jesse to come with me, for starters. Going by myself would be a *really* stupid trick.

"Don't worry, Mom," I whispered as I tiptoed past her room. "I'll be back in no time!"

My sneakers were right where I'd left them, beside the door — still soaked through. I couldn't face putting them on again, so I searched the bottom of the hall closet and finally dug up my mom's black rubber boots. A bit big, but at least my feet would be dry. Then I shuffled through the coats, looking for something dark and waterproof. No luck. My raincoat was shiny red, and my mom's was bright yellow. I grabbed a zippered navy sweatshirt and pulled it on. It wouldn't keep me dry, but it would be one more layer for the rain to get through. On the top shelf, I found a black wool toque. I pulled that on, too. Then I opened the door.

The rain swept in, lashing my face and clothes. The courtyard looked like you could swim in it. I'd be drenched before I even got to the gate.

"Get moving, Stevie," I told myself. The good news was that the downpour would make me less visible. Hunching my shoulders, I stepped out into the night. As I crossed the half-flooded courtyard, I glanced up at Gertie's apartment. A dim light cast a faint glow through her bedroom window. Did I see a movement? A face? I froze. All I could make out was a dim blur behind the thick curtain of rain.

I headed for Jesse's place. Rats! All the windows were dark. Well, what did I expect at three a.m.? I wasn't sure which room was Jesse's, but the window with the baseball decals all over it looked like a pretty good bet. The problem was, how was I going to wake him up without waking his mom, too?

When people in the movies want to wake someone up, they either meow like a cat or throw pebbles against the window.

"Meeoowww," I called. "Meeeoowwww! Meeoooww!"

I waited. Nothing. Then, from behind me, an answering meow. It was the Sebastians' cat, Alexander. He was crouched under a stairway, watching me with huge yellow eyes.

"Mrrroow?" he said. "Mrow?"

Meowing, I decided, was a totally stupid way to wake someone up. Anyway, it wasn't working.

Crawling under the closest bush, I felt around in the dirt and managed to come up with a handful of pebbles. I threw one at Jesse's window, but it hit the wall about three feet too low. The second one didn't hit anything; it just flew up in the air and dropped into a bush. After that, my aim got better. Pebbles 3, 4 and 5 all hit Jesse's window square in the middle and bounced off. I waited, shivering. My sweatshirt was soaked.

"Hurry up, Jesse," I whispered. "I'm freezing out here."

Pebbles 6, 7 and 8 all bounced off the window, and still the bedroom stayed dark. Then I figured it out. The pebbles must sound almost exactly like the raindrops that were beating against the glass. He was *never* going to hear me. Not unless I heaved a full-sized rock through his window.

I had to face it. I was on my own. So now what?

A picture flashed through my mind. My warm dry bed, my soft snuggly quilt.

Then I remembered Loni Matthews, girl detective. Just before all this started, I had been reading *The Mansion with Ghosts in Its Walls*. Loni goes to a haunted house with a gang of her friends, looking for her kidnapped great-aunt. At the very last moment, all her friends chicken out, and she has to search the mansion alone. Does Loni give up?

Absolutely not!

Neither, I decided, would Stevie Diamond.

I crossed the lane to the Red Barn parking lot, empty except for some soggy cartons and a few overflowing garbage cans. The street lights glowed dimly on oily slicks that spread across the pavement like greasy rainbows. As I crept towards the restaurant, I could hear the rooster. *Ruh*-ruh-*ruh*-ruh-*rooooooo* it called through the drumming of the raindrops on the concrete. The *rooooooo* sounded like a dog howling.

The light was coming from the back of the restaurant, where the kitchen was. The windows there were all too small and too high to see through, so I snuck around to the front and leaned against the glass. The dining area was lit by a dim night-light, and I could make out the outlines of tables and counters and cash registers. Empty. I tried to peer into the kitchen, but all I could see was the brightly lit doorway and the light coming through the chute for the burgers.

Moving carefully around the front of the building, I tried the doors. Both locked. That left only the employees' entrance at the back. It led directly into the kitchen. The thief could be right behind the door...watching the knob as it turned.

A bold little voice popped into my brain. I recognized it as the one that usually gets me into trouble. "Do it, Stevie!" it said.

I crept around the building, taking care not to bump into any garbage cans. The rain dripping down my face made me practically blind. I wiped my eyes with the back of my hand. My sweatshirt and toque were soaked. Rainwater ran down my pants and into my mother's rubber boots. When I reached the back door, I stopped, my whole body shivering.

The voice again. "Do it, Stevie!"

I reached for the door. I turned the knob. It moved. There was a click — just the slightest sound. I winced, hoping that the thief hadn't heard it, too. The door gave. Very, very slowly, moving it only a tiny bit at a time, I pushed the door open. When there was room enough in the crack for my head, I edged my face around the door and peered in.

The kitchen was empty—brightly lit by rows of fluorescent lights on the ceiling. The grills and deep fryers gleamed. Boxes of hamburger buns were stacked along one wall. A big plastic container of ketchup stood on the counter beside the chute that led into the dining room. Nobody there.

Maybe the owner had left? But no, the lights were still on. And the door wasn't locked. It didn't make sense. A little voice in my head—a different one this time, kind of timid-sounding—told me to get out of there, to turn right around and run back home as fast as my legs would carry me.

Unfortunately, I didn't listen.

Walking on tiptoe, I crept into the kitchen of the Red Barn. All my senses were alert; I was ready to turn back at any second. It was quiet. So quiet I could hear the refrigerators hum. I moved towards the doorway that led into the front part of the restaurant.

BANG! The kitchen door slammed shut behind me with a sound like an explosion.

I whirled around.

"Well, Stephanie, you just had to push, didn't you? You just *had* to push your luck."

CHAPTER

BEHIND ME—BARRING THE DOOR—STOOD Jonathon. His lips were parted in a smile, but it wasn't his usual big friendly one. It was small and nasty. His purple and blue exercise outfit was spattered with mud, and his white gym shoes were caked with greyish muck.

Just as I thought! I *knew* Jonathon was the thief—it was the wrist-wallet that tipped me off.

Maybe I can fake it, I thought. I just stumbled in here by accident, I don't know anything—

But the look on my face must have been a dead give-away.

"How did you figure out it was me?" he asked. The smile disappeared, and his jaw muscles bulged. "I mean, I know you've been snooping around, but I thought you were after that crazy old lady. Or the big ugly kid who owns the van."

Talk, that was it! If he wanted to talk, maybe I could keep him talking till—

Till what? Who was going to come to the Red Barn at three o'clock in the morning? Still, it was my only chance.

"It wasn't easy," I said slowly. "You covered your tracks pretty well."

"You're right. Nobody suspects a thing."

"Nobody except—" I stopped. Rats! Why did I always have to open my big mouth?

"Except you," he finished, smiling that unfriendly smile again. "Yes, Stephanie. You certainly turned out to be the fly in the ointment, didn't you?"

That's what I felt like. A fly. Stuck in ointment.

"Too bad." He took a step closer. "You see, I spent a lot of time coming up with this plan. A lot of time and work, Stephanie."

"Uh—what plan, Jonathon?" I tried to sound friendly and interested.

"A plan to make me rich," he said quietly. "A plan to make Jonathon Hughes a millionaire."

"A millionaire? Selling hamburgers?"

He scowled. Whoops! Better watch it.

"Ever heard of Ronald McDonald?" he snapped. "Anyhow, they aren't just hamburgers. They're fabulous hamburgers. Everyone says my burgers are the best in town."

"They are!" I said quickly. "No question about it. The best in Vancouver!"

"Ah, but that's the point, Stephanie. Vancouver isn't enough. If you want to become a big national chain—and I do—you have to have a gimmick. Something that'll bring the kids in! It took me months, but I finally came up with it. The best business idea in a decade."

He waited until I finally gave in and asked,

"What business idea?"

"The plastic animals, Stephanie. It was brilliant!" His eyes were glowing now. "Exactly the kind of thing kids love!"

"Jonathon," I stammered, "you've got it wrong. Really, you do. Kids don't want to eat their food out of plastic animals. Maybe they did when you were a kid. But they don't like that stuff any more!"

"What would *you* know about it?" he snorted.

"Jonathon! I'm a kid! I hang out with kids! Why didn't you ask a *kid* before you started making your plastic chickens and pigs?"

"You're wrong. People go for stuff like that. Especially kids! It could be a huge success. I could be the Fast-Food King of Canada. It's perfect!" He stared off into the distance, his eyes shining. Then he glanced back at me and shook his head. "Except for one small problem. Just what am I supposed to do with you, Stephanie?"

"Gosh," I said quickly. "I don't know. How about if I just go home and promise not to tell anyone?"

"Do you think I'm stupid?" He laughed. "You think I'm going to believe that?"

I could see his point. I didn't believe me either.

"To tell you the truth, Stephanie, I don't know what I'm going to do with you. I wish you'd minded your own business. I wish you'd never come here. Now that you have, though . . . " He stared at me, his eyes all cold and squinty like the bad guys in the movies.

I couldn't help it. A little squeak, like a

mouse-squeak, popped out of my mouth.

"So now you're scared. Good! Too bad you weren't scared a couple of days ago when you decided to snoop around. You wouldn't be in all this trouble now, would you?"

I backed up a step. Slowly, so he wouldn't notice.

"How'd you figure it out, kid?" he asked softly. "Might as well tell me. You're not going anywhere." He laid his hand firmly on the doorknob.

"Well," I said, edging my other foot backwards. Keep talking, that was the answer. "I got thrown off at first by the master key. You made it look like the robbery happened while you and my mom were out—like someone got in with a master key." Jonathon nodded and smiled slightly. He seemed to be enjoying this. Good.

"But it didn't happen that way."

He nodded again.

"You invited my mom to go biking." I took another small step backwards. "You knew how slow she is at getting ready to go out. How she dawdles in the front hall for ages, finding her shoes and keys and all. Only a friend would know that." Jonathon smiled, as if he were remembering.

"Right," he said. "I knew all that."

"You knew where the money was because you helped us count it. It must have been easy for you to duck back into the kitchen and grab it. You took the stacks of bills with you when you went biking, didn't you? You put them in

148

your wrist-wallet. But you couldn't take the rolls of coins. You had nowhere to put them."

"Very good, Stephanie," he grinned. "You're right. I had no pockets. You're smarter than you look."

"It was all a trick right from the beginning, wasn't it?" I was talking faster now, and my voice was getting shrill. "You were never my mom's friend at all. You were never really a Garbage Buster. You just joined so you could *spy* on them. So you could mess things up from the inside."

"It was fun," he said. "They're such a bunch of idiots."

"You made those crank phone calls to our house. And you dumped that garbage through our door."

He laughed. "That was the most fun of all."

"And the warning on your door. You did it *yourself*, didn't you? Nobody would suspect you if you had ketchup—or blood—smeared all over your own door."

I edged backwards into the dimly lit dining room. Right at that moment, I wasn't feeling great about my chances. I knew the front doors were locked. The only way out was through the kitchen door, and that was blocked by Jonathon. I was trapped.

"You don't even recycle your garbage," I yelled foolishly. I had backed all the way into the dining room by now and was beginning to feel panicky.

"Oh, horrors! I don't recycle!" sneered Jonathon as he followed me into the dining room. His silhouette in the doorway was backlit from the kitchen. "What are you going to do? Arrest me?"

I had one chance. The hamburger chute behind the counter! It led into the kitchen. If I could just reach it, I could—maybe—crawl through and race for the back door.

Jonathon must have seen me looking at the chute. He lunged forward to grab me just as I made a dash for the counter. I guess he fell—I heard a crash behind me. By the time he got up, I could have been—should have been—out the door.

It was my boots! When I tried to run, they slopped around, half falling off. Kicking hard, I ran right out of them and jumped over the counter, landing right in front of the chute. I leaped up and got a handhold, scrambling in. I was halfway through when I felt the hand on my ankle.

"Stephanie, come back! I just want to talk!"

Hah!

"I won't hurt you. Come back!"

"Let go, you creep!" I kicked at the hand holding my ankle, but he had a solid grip. I managed to pull my head over the top of the chute into the kitchen. I looked around. What could I throw back at him?

Holding on to the top of the chute with one hand, I grabbed at the plastic jar of ketchup with the other. It was heavy, but I got a grip on it. Just as I hoisted it up to hurl it down the chute, the lid flew off. Bang, clang—it clattered noisily down the ramp.

Behind the lid came...ketchup! Everywhere! From my forehead down to my toes. My hands were so slippery I lost my grip on the big plastic jar. It bounced down the ramp and—I think— hit Jonathon. I heard him swear.

The hand on my ankle loosened, and I started climbing again. I couldn't see anything now. The ketchup was everywhere, all over the chute, all over me. No way to get a grip. I scrambled up and slid back, scrambled and slid. The hand on my ankle tightened again. My slippery hands were losing their hold on the top of the chute. I could feel myself sliding backwards...

That's when I heard the voice, coming from the kitchen doorway. "Hold it right there, buddy!" it said roughly. "Let go of the kid!"

CHAPTER

THE HAND CAME OFF MY ANKLE SO SUDDENLY that my foot sprang up in the air. I slid slowly back down the chute. As soon as I landed, I wiped the ketchup off my face and peered into the doorway.

It was Eyebrows—the strange old guy who'd been watching me at the demonstration, the one Jesse thought was my grandfather! In his hand was a small revolver. It was pointed straight at Jonathon.

"Take it easy!" said Jonathon, raising his hands. He was covered in ketchup, just like me. Red didn't go so hot with his aerobics suit. "No need for any unpleasantness here. I'm sure we can all just talk this over."

"Get on the phone, kid!" Eyebrows ordered. I was *positive* I'd heard that voice before. "Call 911. Tell them to send the cop squad. And tell them to make it fast!"

"Right!" If Eyebrows was rescuing me from Jonathon, I was happy to take orders. There was a phone in the kitchen, right next to the grill. I stepped carefully, since my feet were all slippery with ketchup and there was a huge puddle of water on the kitchen floor, where I'd stood, dripping, earlier.

I dialled as fast as I could. After I had stammered out my story, the voice on the other end told me that a police car was on its way. As I hung up the phone, I took a good look at Eyebrows. There was definitely something funny about this guy. Not just that green and brown suit, although it was pretty weird and old-fashioned.

His hair! It was on crooked. Sort of falling over one ear.

Okay. So Eyebrows was wearing a wig. Maybe he was bald and sensitive about it. Lots of old guys are bald and maybe sensitive about it.

But there was something else. Something about his shape. It was peculiar and somehow familiar—

Then I realized. The old man was pear-shaped!

"Gertie!" I yelled.

She turned. Or he turned. Or whatever! At the same moment, Jonathon's arms dropped. He pushed past Gertie and dived past me, heading for the door.

Guess he didn't notice the puddle.

His feet flew so high in the air he practically did a somersault. The crash when he landed shook the building. He sprawled there for a few seconds, groaning, while Gertie and I watched, too surprised to move. Then he got to his knees and lunged for the door, knocking over three boxes of hamburger buns on his way. He was reaching for the door when it flew open.

Arnie. And Slug. Their thick hulking figures blocked the doorway. Rain dripped down their faces.

"You okay, Gertie?" Arnie called out. Crossing his arms across his chest, he stared down at Jonathon, who was propped against a stack of boxes.

Gertie pulled off the moustache and eyebrows, and dropped her gun on the counter. "Arnie," she grinned, "you sure do have a terrific sense of timing."

The police, when they arrived, turned out to be the same two police officers who had been at my house earlier that evening — the sandy-haired woman and the tall, bald man.

"What? You again?" said the woman, staring at me. "What on earth *happened* to you?"

I looked down. I was red and sticky from one end to the other. There was a pool of red goo under my stockinged feet. "Uh...ketchup," I said. "I, uh, spilled a bit."

"Uh-huh," said the policewoman. Then she looked over at Gertie and frowned. I could see why. Gertie's face was covered in strange make-up, with funny white strips where the moustache and eyebrows had been. The grey wig was hanging half off and half on.

"Here!" I pointed at Jonathon. "This is the bad guy. Right here! Arrest him!"

Jonathon stood up unsteadily. "Officers," he said, "I am the owner of this establishment. I would like to report a break-in. I caught these people—all of them—in the act of vandalizing my restaurant." He was trying to look business-like, which isn't easy when you have a big blob of ketchup on your nose.

The police officers looked from Jonathon to Gertie to me. Then they looked at Arnie, who shook his head and shrugged. Slug just laughed. The police looked confused. I didn't blame them.

The policeman crossed the kitchen and picked up Gertie's gun from the counter. "Okay," he said. "Let's start with this. Which one of you does this belong to?"

Gertie slowly raised her hand. "That's...uh...mine, Officer."

The policeman pointed the gun at the floor and pulled the trigger. A bright red flag popped out. "BANG," it said.

"Very funny," said the policewoman. "Now who called 911?"

Before I could answer, the door flew open again and Jesse charged in—striped pyjamas dripping, sneakers half falling off. Right behind him came my mom. Her blue terry-cloth bathrobe was soaked, and her fuzzy slippers were spattered with mud. She looked frantic.

"Stee-veeee!" she screeched. "What *happened* to you?"

155

"Mom, it's ketchup! Just ketchup. I spilled a jar — when I was — before — Mom, it's just ketchup!"

"Ohhhh," she moaned, collapsing against a wall. "You're going to be the death of me..."

"Stevie, how *could* you?" said Jesse. "How could you come over here without telling me?"

"I didn't," I said. "I mean, I tried. I threw stones and meowed and — "

"I don't mean to interrupt," said the policewoman, "but do you suppose we could all sit down somewhere and try to get to the bottom of this?"

The whole story came out in the dining room. I told some, and Gertie told some, and when my mom started to figure it out, she told the rest. She kept staring at Jonathon and saying "Jonathon, I can't believe it!" and "Jonathon, how could you?" and finally, "Jonathon, you rat!" Jonathon tried to stick to his story of all of us breaking into the restaurant, but no one believed him.

Me, I was still pretty stunned and confused. "What were you doing, Gertie? Why did you dress up like that?"

"Oh, well," she said. "I used to be an actress, you see. Long before you were born. A good one, too." She stared out the window, like she was remembering.

"Yeah?" I said. "So?"

"So, I miss it sometimes," she said. "When you came barging into my place that day, you told me about this detective stuff. Sounded

156

dangerous to me, so I decided to keep an eye on you. But every time I came near, you ran like a rabbit."

"Oh." I was seriously embarrassed. "Yeah, I guess I did."

"I could see you weren't going to let me within a mile of you. So I needed a disguise. This here was my costume from *Murder In The Shoe Store*. I played the detective," she said proudly. "Harry Snell."

"A detective?" I said. "Wow! But how come you played a man?"

"Wartime, you see. All the men gone off to war. I played a lot of men's roles in those days." She stared off into space again. "Even Hamlet, once."

"So that's what that stuff is!" said Jesse.

"What stuff?" Gertie stared around, confused.

"The stuff in your china cabinet. The eyeball and the pot of blood and the funny little sticks. It's stage make-up, right?"

Gertie stared at him as if he wasn't too bright. "Of course," she said. "What else would it be?"

"And the dagger and the gun?" he went on.

"Props. I saved them as souvenirs. And, say..." Gertie stared hard at Jesse, "how come you know what's in my china cabinet? You've never been in my place, have you?"

I figured this was a good time to interrupt. "What I don't understand is how you guys knew where I was. All of you. How did you know I was here?"

They looked at each other. Gertie said, "Well,

I'll go first. I don't sleep well these days, you see. Part of getting old. I saw you out there in the courtyard with your pebbles. Heard you meowing."

"Meowing?" said Jesse. "Really? You were meowing?"

"Never mind," I said. "I'll explain later."

"Anyhow, when I saw you sneaking over to the Red Barn, I got worried. I decided it was time for Harry Snell to put in an appearance. And just in case Harry couldn't handle it on his own, I put a call through to my friend Arnie." She turned and patted Arnie's hand. He smiled back.

"Okay," I said. "That explains Gertie, Slug and Arnie. But what about you, Mom? How did you know I was here?"

"Well, something woke me up and—"

"Woke you up? You sleep like a log."

"Maybe it was your silly meowing. Or mother's intuition. How do I know? Anyhow, I checked your room and discovered you were gone. Stevie, you nearly frightened me to death. I thought you must have slipped out to see Jesse and—"

"And so she came to my place," Jesse continued. "She told me you were gone. You'd been going on and on about the Red Barn so much, I knew you must be here."

"Well!" interrupted Jonathon. "Now that you're all congratulating each other, why don't you congratulate yourselves on ruining my business!"

My mom's voice was quiet. "Nobody wanted to ruin your business, Jonathon. We only wanted you to be a little more responsible about how you ran it."

There was a loud banging on the kitchen door, and two more people walked in—a man with a tape recorder and a woman with a bunch of cameras around her neck.

"Vancouver Tribune," said the man. "Police headquarters tells us there was a robbery here tonight?"

"Not here," said Jesse. "And not tonight either. The robbery was days ago. At her house." He pointed at me.

The reporter sat down, set up his tape recorder and pulled out a pen and note pad. "Let's start with your name," he said.

"Stevie," I said proudly. "Stevie Olivia Diamond."

Half an hour later, we all headed back to the co-op. Except for Jonathon. He went off with the police, for further questioning. It was still raining, but I was past caring. I was sure I'd never be dry again in my whole life. Suddenly I stopped short.

"Wait a minute!" I said. "Arnie Sykes! You better explain something. What were you doing with all those plastic Cluck Burger packages? And those chicken feet? And all those feathers?"

"Yeah," said Jesse. "What were you doing

with that stuff?"

"Stee-veee!" my mom said, shivering in her bathrobe. "Can't this wait? We're all going to get pneumonia."

"I got a question of my own," said Arnie. "What were you two doing in my van today?"

"What?" My mom stared at Arnie, then at Jesse and finally at me. "What's going on here? Stevie, you told me—"

"Oh, now, now," said Gertie, taking my hand in her left hand and Arnie's in her right and walking us in the direction of the co-op. "Arnie's an art student, Stevie. He does very... interesting art, using rather unusual materials."

"Chicken feet?"

"I *said* they were unusual," said Gertie. "He's working on a series right now, aren't you, Arnie?"

"Uh, yeah," said Arnie. "It's called 'Dead Birds in Flight.'"

"It sounds just wonderful," said Gertie, as we walked through the courtyard gate. "I can hardly wait to see it."

CHAPTER

AT SCHOOL THE NEXT DAY, WE WERE FAMOUS. The early edition of the *Tribune* had a huge picture of Jesse and me on its front page. Jesse looked great in his striped pyjamas, grinning about as wide as his mouth would go. Me? I was covered in so much ketchup, I looked like a French fry. Fortunately, the picture wasn't in colour. Underneath, it said "Eleven-Year-Olds Foil Fast-Food Fraud." Below that, in smaller letters, it said "Burger Business Blown by Young Detectives."

All the kids in my class were whispering and showing each other newspapers when I walked in. The room went silent for a minute, and then the questions started flying.

"Hey, cool! Were you really covered in ketchup?"

"Weren't you scared?"

"How come they call you Stevie in the paper? I thought your name was Stephanie."

Ms. Wootechuk appeared in the doorway. "I'm sure we all want to hear about Stephanie's—*Stevie's*—big adventure," she interrupted with a smile. "Why don't we skip our study of the spider for today? We'll ask Stevie to give us a first-hand report on what happened at the Red Barn last night, instead."

She sat down at her desk, looking as eager as the kids. "Now, Stevie," she said. "Start at the very beginning. Tell us every single little detail. Don't skip a thing!"

Amazing! I had no idea that Ms. Wootechuk was a mystery fan. You never can tell, can you? And on the day the spider diagram was due, too. I shoved my unfinished diagram to the back of my desk, folded my hands on top and began. "It all started the day I came home and found my mom crying..."

Everyone shut right up. They all leaned forward in their desks to listen. I could tell I was going to enjoy being famous.

A week later—on a Saturday—my mom had a big pot-luck brunch for all the people who had offered to look for Jesse and me when they *thought* we were lost. She kept talking about how great our friends and neighbours had been. She also said she had a big surprise for me. I was hoping it wasn't a speech I'd have to make, thanking everyone for rescuing me when I wasn't even lost in the first place.

My mom made a big pot of—yuck!—curried garbanzo beans with—double yuck!—pieces of eggplant floating around in it. Thanks to me, however, our family contribution wasn't totally gross. I made a huge chocolate cake covered in chocolate icing with sprinkles and jujubes. It sagged a little bit in the middle, but not so you'd notice. I stuck it in a cupboard till dessert time.

Jesse and his mom arrived first with a big mushroom-and-spinach quiche, and Gertie was right behind them with a fruit-and-nut loaf. She brought Herb Crum with her. He was carrying a package of white buns from Safeway. Maisie Sebastian showed up with some salmon pâté and crackers, and the Wongs brought some delicious-smelling deep-fried things. Wilma and Pete turned up with a macaroni-and-cheese casserole *and* a plate of cookies.

I love pot lucks!

We were starting to eat when the doorbell rang again, and Arnie walked in, carrying this huge tray piled high with tropical fruit. Mangoes and bananas and papayas on the bottom, thick pineapple slices in the middle, and kiwi fruit and grapes on top. It looked like a pyramid and was so gorgeous, I was convinced — Arnie *must* be an artist. He just stood there in the doorway till my mom came and took the tray, and then he kind of slid into a chair beside the door, without even taking his jacket off. I could see his T-shirt, though. It said "Angel of Death."

"Arnie's shy," Gertie whispered in my ear. "He was kind of nervous about coming today. I'll just go over and talk to him awhile."

Arnie? Shy? How could you look like *that* and be shy?

"Stevie?" It was Mrs. Kulniki. She was standing by the stove, making coffee. "Come on over here. I've got a special treat for you." She opened the oven door and pulled something out with an oven mitt. "Jesse tells me that this is your favourite food in the whole world."

She was holding a china plate. On it were three — count 'em, three! — Cluck Burgers. Fabulous Sauce dripped out the sides. Steam rose from the buns and floated up into my nose...ahhhhhhh.

"Careful, now," Mrs. Kulniki said with a smile. "The plate's hot."

I took a big bite and then remembered something. "Mrs. Kulniki? What's going to happen now? At the Red Barn, I mean." I wondered if she was going to lose her job.

"Didn't Jesse tell you the news?"

"What news?" Jesse wandered over, holding a half-eaten brownie in one hand and a piece of pineapple in the other.

"About Jonathon selling the restaurant," she said.

"What?" I sputtered. "How? To who?"

"You sound like an owl, Stevie," said Jesse. "Jonathon is selling the Red Barn back to the Smithers family."

"The Smithers family! But I thought Jonathon bought it from them."

"Well, yeah, he did," said Jesse. "But he never told them about the plastic animals and wanting it to be a huge chain."

"The Smithers' grandfather started that

restaurant," said Mrs. Kulniki, "and he built it up very slowly and carefully. When Jonathon started to change everything, the rest of the family realized how much the Red Barn meant to them."

"So when Jonathon decided to sell—" continued Jesse.

"Sell?" I asked. "Why?"

"Because of you, I imagine," said Mrs. Kulniki. "And the Garbage Busters, of course. Business was already falling off because of the Garbage Busters' demonstrations. And now, since that newspaper article—well, people are totally avoiding the place. Especially kids."

"Really?" I said. "No kids?"

"Well, I sure haven't seen many," said Mrs. Kulniki, "and the Red Barn counts on their business."

"I know," I said, remembering what Jonathon had said about kid customers. Problem was, he knew even less about kids than I knew about spider parts.

"Anyway," said Mrs. Kulniki, "he's had it with the restaurant. He wants to start a physical fitness studio instead. The Smithers family is buying him out and putting everything back the way it was."

"No more plastic animals?"

"No more plastic animals."

I looked at my Cluck Burgers. Two left, but I could picture a future where they stretched into the distance forever—as far as the eye could see.

"And you'll keep your job?" I asked Mrs. Kulniki.

"I don't see why not. I fry a mean Cluck Burger. Oh, gosh! I guess they won't be Cluck Burgers any more. They'll go back to being Fabulous Chicken Burgers."

Something soft was rubbing against my leg. Radical purred at me in a coaxing kind of way. *Oh, come on, you don't need both those burgers, do you?* I slipped him half a chicken patty. He slipped me a big cat-smile.

My mom came up and gave me a hug. "Isn't it great news, sweetie? About the Red Barn?"

"Yeah," I said, biting into the third Cluck Burger. "So what's going to happen to Jonathon?"

"We've already worked it out," said my mom. "He doesn't want any more trouble or bad publicity. He's offered to pay the money back and give the Garbage Busters an extra two thousand dollars — for damages. The police have agreed not to press charges as long as he pays up."

"Two thousand dollars!" said Jesse. "Wow!"

"We can really use it," said Wilma. "And we'll take it. Even from a rat!"

"Is he still going to live in the co-op?" I asked. I wasn't crazy about running into him in the courtyard or laundry room.

"I doubt it," said Mrs. Kulniki. "People are on to him now. My guess is he'll be gone by the end of the month."

"Psst! Stevie!"

166

It was Gertie. Across the room.

"Excuse me," I said, and went over. "What's up, Gertie?"

"C'mon," she said. "I want to show you something—at my place. But I don't want to drag the whole kit and caboodle along."

"What is it?" I asked, as we crossed the courtyard.

"Birthday present," she mumbled.

"Gee, thanks, Gertie," I said. "But it's not my birthday."

"Of course not, you silly wazoo! It's *my* birthday."

"Really? Wow! How old are you, Gertie?"

"Oh, not too old," she said. "Just seventy-two."

"Seventy-two!" I couldn't stop myself from adding, "That's not old?"

"No," said Gertie firmly. "When you get to be my age, you'll understand. Now, ninety! That's old!"

When we got to Gertie's apartment, she told me to close my eyes. Then she led me through the door.

"Okay," she said. "Take a gander at that! My present from Arnie!"

My eyes opened. My jaw dropped. "I don't believe it!"

It was a huge painting. Big enough to cover most of one wall. A collage, I guess, made up of a whole lot of different stuff. Right in the middle was the Red Barn rooster. It was almost as big as me, and it was standing in its cracked egg and crowing into the air. The egg was made out of real pieces of eggshell. Arnie must have boiled and peeled *hundreds* of eggs to get all those eggshells. And the rooster was made out of all kinds of real feathers—from huge bright peacock feathers to tiny white down feathers. Its comb was made out of a red rubber glove, and its beak was a pair of old scissors.

But the amazing thing was this. Crowded into the sky above the rooster were at least a dozen life-sized chickens. Made out of real feathers. And with real chicken feet, just like the ones in Arnie's van. They looked very lifelike, except for two things: Number one, they were flying— which, you have to admit, most chickens just can't do. And number two, their heads looked very, very familiar. They just happened, in fact, to exactly match three plastic chicken heads that were sitting on top of my dresser right this minute. My prize clues!

"It's called 'Chickens in Flight'!" Gertie said. "Arnie did it."

"Gertie," I said, "that's just about the coolest picture I've ever seen."

"You really like it?"

"I love it!"

"Me, too. Freddy's not crazy about it, though." She pointed over to her cockatoo, who squawked unhappily. He looked about as annoyed as a cockatoo can look.

❖ ❖ ❖

Back at the pot luck, I told Jesse about the painting.

"He's using real bird feathers and real bird feet to make his dumb pictures?" Jesse spluttered. "That's disgusting! It's gross! It's—"

"Don't get mad at me," I said. "Why don't you go tell Arnie? He's sitting right there."

Jesse gulped, and his eyes got big. "He'd kill me. He'd reach out one big hairy paw and smash me into the ground."

"Oh, go on," I said. "He's not as bad as he looks."

"I hope not," said Jesse. "Because he looks *real* bad."

Jesse wandered slowly across the room. A few minutes later, he was talking to Arnie. At first, Jesse looked kind of shy and awkward. Soon, though, he started getting all worked up—the way he sometimes gets. After a while, Arnie started glancing nervously from side to side. He even started edging towards the door.

"What's going on there?" asked Gertie. "Is Jesse picking on poor Arnie?"

I grinned. "Sort of."

Then I remembered—Gertie's birthday! I went into the kitchen and pulled my cake out of the cupboard. I found candles in a drawer, but there were only twenty of them. Never mind—seventy-two would probably set the cake on fire anyway. I settled for a group of seven and a group of two.

"Happy birthday to you," I sang as I carried the cake into the living room. By the time I reached Gertie, everyone had joined in. Gertie looked thrilled to bits.

She had just finished cutting the cake when the doorbell rang.

"Can you get it, Stevie?" my mom said. "It might be your surprise."

The door opened, and this goofy-looking guy was standing there, wearing jeans and a red-and-black checked jacket. His hair was sticking up and looked like it hadn't been combed in a week.

"Dad!" I yelled, crossing the room in two bounds and jumping into his arms. He smelled like leaves and wood-smoke and fresh air. My mom was right behind me, and soon the three of us were in a big bunch, hugging and laughing.

"You're here!" I yelled. "You came!"

"Well, of course, I came," said my dad. "When I heard that Valerie was *delirious* about some guy named Jonathon, I figured I'd better get back here." He grinned at my mom and planted a big kiss on her cheek.

"Delirious!" she said sharply. "Stevie! What kind of nonsense have you been telling your father?"

"Oops," I said. "Did I say delirious? I meant to say *furious*. Mom's been furious ever since she found out what Jonathon's been up to. Say, Dad," I continued, leading him away from my mom and over to the food table, "have you ever tried Mom's terrific curried garbanzo beans?"

"You're not going to get away that easily," my mom said. "Your dad told me what you said about Jonathon and me. Why on earth did you think I was — good heavens! — in love with Jonathon?"

I squirmed. "I don't know," I said. "He was so friendly all the time and so...handsome."

"Jonathon? Handsome?" My mom looked surprised. "Don't be silly, Stevie. Your dad is *much* more handsome than Jonathon."

"Dad? Are you kidding?"

"Hey!" said Dad. He turned his face sideways. "Take a look at that profile. Have you ever seen a better-looking guy in your whole life?"

His brown hair stuck straight up, his long nose stuck straight out, and he had this stupid-looking grin on his face. He looked ridiculous. "You look good, Dad," I laughed.

"Good?"

"Okay, okay. Handsome."

"Just handsome?"

"Gorgeous," I said. "Beautiful."

My dad looked at my mom.

"Breathtaking," she said with a smile. "Dazzling."

"You bet your bippy I am!" He grabbed us both into a hug. "Runs in the Diamond family."

We introduced my dad to everybody, and then we took him on a guided tour of the town house. "It's great, Dad," I told him. "Nice place. Nice people. You're going to love it here. Are you back for good?"

"Well, for a while. I've got to write up my findings. But then I've got a job in the bush starting in February."

171

"What?" I said. "You're kidding. No fair."

"No, I guess it's not," said my dad. "But, honey, I've got to earn some money to finish my research. I'll be helping to run a tree-planting camp up in the northern part of Vancouver Island."

"Rats!" I said. I wanted to say something worse. Swear even.

"Stevie, it's months away. Not till February. Besides, there's no reason why you couldn't come out and join me for a while. You could be a big help."

"And miss school?" I looked at my mom.

"You could take some school work along," she said slowly. "I think it would be good for you."

"Fantastic!"

When I told Jesse what my dad had said, his eyes lit up. "We just *have* to figure out a way for me to go, too," he said.

I stepped back, surprised. "You mean, you want to?"

"Of course! We're partners, aren't we? There'd be grizzly bears up there and wild cats. I could rescue—"

"You could what?" I asked.

"We could rescue *each other*," he said quickly, holding out his hand. We shook on it.

My mom and dad strolled back into the kitchen just then, with their arms around each other's waists. They looked sort of—there was no other word—delirious about each other. When my dad saw me and Jesse, he snapped his fingers as if he'd just remembered something. Then he started rummaging through his knapsack.

"I've got something for you two," he said, pulling two small boxes out of his pack. "A friend of mine did a rush job on these." He handed a box to each of us.

I opened mine first.

STEVIE DIAMOND

Diamond & Kulniki Detective Agency
2025 9th Avenue
Vancouver, B. C.
555-7331

No mystery too tough for us!

Business cards! Zillions of them.

"Stevie, look!" said Jesse. His cards looked like this:

JESSE KULNIKI

Kulniki & Diamond Detective Agency
2033 9th Avenue
Vancouver, B. C.
555-4046

No mystery too tough for us!

"Wow!" said Jesse.

"There are only five hundred per box," said my dad. "But we can always reorder when you run out."

"Wow!" said Jesse. "My very first business cards."

Mrs. Kulniki came over and smiled when she saw the cards. "I'm sure it will be a wonderful career, Jesse," she said, "and we'll all be very proud of you two. Just as long as you tell us where you're going!"

"And for how long," my mom added.

"And who with," Mrs. Kulniki said.

"And *not* in the middle of the night," said my dad.

Jesse groaned. I rolled my eyes.

"Anything else?" I asked sarcastically.

"Yeah. Like maybe we could wear beepers or something," said Jesse. "That way, you could tell where we are every single second of every single day."

"That would be very nice," said my mom.

"Perfect!" said Mrs. Kulniki, nodding.

"Well, it would certainly satisfy *me*," said my dad.

We all broke out laughing.

"Say, Dad," I said, "are there ever any mysterious goings-on in tree-planting camps? Any strange events that need investigating?"

"Are you kidding?" He laughed. "Absolutely everything in a tree-planting camp is strange. Why? You planning on doing some detecting next spring?"

"Well," I said, "I'm not used to investigating mysteries all by myself. You see, I have this partner—"

"Uh, oh," said my mom.

"Oh, dear," said Mrs. Kulniki.

"Both of you?" asked my dad.

Jesse and I just smiled.

This was only the beginning...

ABOUT THE AUTHOR

Linda Bailey was a cautious child who never would have dared to do the things Stevie does. She lives in Vancouver and still hasn't found any clues in her garbage.

Other books in the Stevie Diamond Mystery series:

How Can I Be a Detective If I Have to Baby-sit?
Who's Got Gertie? And How Can We Get Her Back!